WESTERN WP PROMISES

SHIPMENT 5

Rodeo Daddy by Marin Thomas
His Medicine Woman by Stella Bagwell
A Real Live Cowboy by Judy Duarte
Wyatt's Ready-Made Family by Patricia Thayer
The Cowboy Code by Christine Wenger
A Rancher's Pride by Barbara White Daille

SHIPMENT 6

Cowboy Be Mine by Tina Leonard
Big Sky Bride, Be Mine! by Victoria Pade
Hard Case Cowboy by Nina Bruhns
Texas Heir by Linda Warren
Bachelor Cowboy by Roxann Delaney
The Forgotten Cowboy by Kara Lennox
The Prodigal Texan by Lynnette Kent

SHIPMENT 7

The Bull Rider's Secret by Marin Thomas
Lone Star Daddy by Stella Bagwell
The Cowboy and the Princess by Myrna Mackenzie
Dylan's Last Dare by Patricia Thayer
Made for a Texas Marriage by Crystal Green
Cinderella and the Cowboy by Judy Christenberry

SHIPMENT 8

Samantha's Cowboy by Marin Thomas
Cowboy at the Crossroads by Linda Warren
Rancher and Protector by Judy Christenberry
Texas Trouble by Kathleen O'Brien
Vegas Two-Step by Liz Talley
A Cowgirl's Secret by Laura Marie Altom

WESTERN WP PROMISES

A Bride for a Blue-Ribbon Cowboy

USA TODAY Bestselling Author

JUDY DUARTE

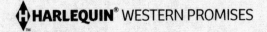

HARLEQUIN® WESTERN PROMISES

Recycling programs
for this product may
not exist in your area.

ISBN-13: 978-0-373-00329-7

A Bride for a Blue-Ribbon Cowboy

Copyright © 2005 by Judy Duarte

Printed in U.S.A.

USA TODAY bestselling author **Judy Duarte** couldn't shake the dream of creating a story of her own. That dream became a reality in 2002 when Harlequin released the first of more than thirty-five of her books. Judy's stories have touched the hearts of readers around the world. A two-time RITA® Award finalist, Judy's books have won two MAGGIE® Awards and a National Readers' Choice Award. You can contact her at judyduarte.com or on Facebook at Facebook.com/judyduartenovelist.

Books by Judy Duarte

Harlequin Special Edition

Return to Brighton Valley
The Bachelor's Brighton Valley Bride
The Daddy Secret

The Fortunes of Texas: Welcome to Horseback Hollow
A House Full of Fortunes!

The Fortunes of Texas: Southern Invasion
Marry Me, Mendoza

Byrds of a Feather
Tammy and the Doctor

Brighton Valley Babies
The Cowboy's Family Plan
The Rancher's Hired Fiancée
A Baby Under the Tree

The Fortunes of Texas: Whirlwind Romance
Mendoza's Miracle

Brighton Valley Medical Center
Race to the Altar
His, Hers and...Theirs?
Under the Mistletoe with John Doe

Visit the Author Profile page at Harlequin.com for more titles.

To Chad Duarte, who has been a good sport about his mother's writing career—most of the time. In spite of what you might occasionally think, Mom doesn't love her computer more than she loves you.

Chapter One

When Blake Gray Feather agreed to compete in the upcoming rodeo, the Blossom County Fair Board had practically danced in the town square.

After all, Blake's fame and his local-boy status would bring in the crowd—and the revenue—they desperately needed. And since the rodeo was the kick-off to the fair, they hoped the community enthusiasm and attendance would carry over.

But Cindy Tucker had her own reasons to be excited. The good-looking cowboy with the rebel grin would be staying at the Tumbling T with her and Grandpa for a couple of weeks.

And that's all she needed to put her plan into motion—a plan that had been stewing since the first of the year. Or maybe even beyond that, if truth be told.

Several times throughout the morning, she'd wandered into the living room, peered out the big bay window and searched the long graveled driveway that led to the ranch house.

But Blake had yet to show up.

She really ought to be helping Grandpa fix the south fence, but she'd been so eager to see Blake that she'd puttered around the house all morning, doing the odd jobs she'd been neglecting. But at least she'd finally fixed that leaky valve in the toilet tank and replaced the lightbulb in the hall closet. And now she was removing the cracked P-trap under the kitchen sink.

As she adjusted the wrench, Shep, the cattle dog, barked, then got up from where he'd plopped onto the kitchen floor and trotted into the living room.

Had Shep heard Blake's truck?

Cindy set down the tool and climbed out from under the sink.

Yep. That was definitely an approaching vehicle. She brushed her hands against her denim-clad hips and hurried to the front door, where she spotted a black truck pulling a fancy horse trailer and kicking up dust as it headed toward the house.

Recognizing the driver, she blew out the breath she'd been holding. Gosh, it was good to have Blake home in Blossom. And for more than a quick visit.

Ever since he'd come to live on the ranch as a teenager, he'd become part of the family.

Of course, as a ten-year-old who'd had her grandpa to herself for five whole years, Cindy hadn't been too happy when fourteen-year-old Blake had first arrived. He'd been a surly adolescent in need of her grandfather's guidance and a real thorn in her backside. But over the next few months, he'd evolved into a friend. And by the time he was ready to move on, he'd become the occasional romantic lead in the midnight dreams of a goofy preteen.

But that was just between Cindy and her pillow.

Blake, who'd always been a ladies man, was *way* out of a tomboy's league—at least in a romantic sense.

But Cindy had a big favor she intended to ask of him, a favor she'd cooked up right after finding out he was coming home to stay for a while. And she wasn't beyond begging, either.

Unless, of course, he teased her about it. Then she'd be fighting mad.

She swung open the front door, letting Shep dash outside with his tail a-waggin' like crazy and barking to beat the band. But Cindy stood just inside the house, watching as Blake got out of a black, dual-axle Chevy pickup wearing a white shirt, black Wranglers and an expensive pair of boots.

Boy howdy, that man was a looker. The kind that made a girl or a woman take a second gawk.

And a third.

He'd inherited the absolute best his German and Comanche bloodlines had to offer. And eight years on his own, riding the rodeo circuit, had hardened the boy right out of him and announced him all grown-up and more handsome than ever.

As he shut the driver's door, he adjusted his black Stetson, allowing the afternoon sunlight to glisten off coal-black strands of hair.

Shep howled, and when Blake glanced at the doorway and spotted Cindy, he slid her a heart-stopping grin. "Hey, Sprout. What's up?"

"Not much." She stood rooted in the doorway, fighting the urge to race outside and give him a great big hug—like she'd always done when she was younger. But now that she had reached the ripe old age of twenty-two and gotten a new attitude about a few things, she wanted him to see her as a woman, and not the awkward little red-haired girl of his youth.

He carried himself with that lean, cowboy swagger and sauntered toward the porch, looking like a buckle bunny's dream come true. And hers, too, if her pillow could talk.

Blake gave Shep a hearty rubdown, then looked up at Cindy. "Hey, aren't you going to give me a welcome-home hug?"

"Sure." She pushed open the screen door, letting it slam behind her, and met him halfway.

As she tiptoed and wrapped him in a warm embrace, she savored the feel of his arms around her, the musky masculine scent of cologne that smelled as brisk and fresh as a mountain stream.

She couldn't help wondering if Robby Bradshaw's hug would feel as nice. She hoped and prayed it would, but doubt niggled at her.

Still, she knew better than to let her imagination get away from her. Some crushes, like the ones teenyboppers had on Hollywood movie stars and rock musicians, were just dreams to carry a young girl until someone more suitable came along. Someone who wasn't out of reach and who would be happy to remain in Blossom and raise a family.

Someone like Robby.

As Blake released her, those whiskey-brown eyes that had always mesmerized her—if she'd let them—glimmered with sincerity. "You're looking good."

"Thanks." But she knew the difference between looking good and being pretty.

Which brought her to the subject she wanted to broach. All she had to do was figure out how to slide it into the conversation as if it belonged there.

As Blake strode toward the fancy horse trailer that looked brand-new, he said, "You have no idea how badly I need a little peace and quiet. I'm really looking forward to my stay here as a much-needed vacation."

"Good." She was glad he'd be around for a while. Well, *thrilled* was more like it. In the past, he'd only come for brief visits. So two weeks seemed like forever to her, and it ought to be plenty of time for what she had in mind.

She watched as he unloaded a chestnut gelding, the kind of mount a skilled cowboy deserved. "That's a fine-looking horse."

"Thanks. He's one of the best cutting horses in all of Texas. His name is Cutter."

She nibbled on her bottom lip as she tried to rustle up the courage to spring her request on him.

"Blake, I…uh…want to ask you a favor."

"Sure. What is it?"

That was easy enough. It sounded as if he'd made a commitment to help, and she hadn't even told him yet.

"Last winter, when Robby Bradshaw was home for Christmas break, I ran into him at Twin Oaks Lake, where he was fishing. And he…uh…" Ah, shoot. Robby hadn't exactly spit out the words, yet somehow, she'd figured out what was on his mind. And his obvious interest in her had set off a flurry of excitement.

Blake's movements stilled. He tensed and his brow furrowed. His eyes hardened. "What the hell did that guy do to you?"

"Oh, no," she said, realizing he might feel the need to defend her honor or something, although it was kind of nice to think that he might, if she needed him to. "It's just that he sort of…well, he's in Colorado and will be graduating from CSU soon, and we're probably going to go out on a date. And stuff."

"A date and *stuff?*" Blake arched a brow in a big-brotherly way.

She kicked at the ground with the scuffed toe of her boot. "Well, it's not like I have a ton of experience with men or with romance. You ought to know that. So I could use a little coaching on how to act around him. And since you're such an expert on...well, that sort of thing, I figured you'd make a perfect tutor."

Blake couldn't help the grin that stole across his face. Little Cindy Lou, with her red hair wrapped into a knot on her head, her flannel shirt rolled to her forearms and a black smudge across her freckled nose, was growing up. And she wanted him to give her some pointers about men.

She crossed her arms and shifted her weight to one foot. "Don't laugh."

"I'm not laughing. I'm just glad to see that you're finally interested in the opposite sex. That's all."

"You, of all people, ought to know how tough it is for me. I can hardly remember my mother, let alone my grandmother."

"I know that, honey."

She'd never had too many girlfriends, either. Blake had never been sure if that was because she was stubborn and difficult to get along with, or if she felt some damn obligation to stick close to her grandpa and the ranch. Before Blake had come to live with them, the old rodeo cowboy and his granddaughter had been close. And more than once, Blake had suspected that Cindy had wanted to be the son Tuck had lost when her daddy died.

It hadn't taken Blake five minutes on the Tumbling T to realize the red-haired girl was a dedicated tomboy. But then again, maybe that was because she didn't stand a chance of developing into a lady and knew it.

Benjamin "Tuck" Tucker was a darn good cowboy. And he'd done a fine job straightening out Blake, a troubled teenage boy who'd been shipped off by his own grandfather to live on the Tumbling T. But Tuck didn't know squat about raising little girls. So it wasn't any wonder Cindy was a bit backward when it came to womanly things, like cooking and sewing, primping and flirting.

"So what do you say?" she asked.

He countered with a question of his own. "What would you have done if I hadn't come back home?"

She crossed her arms and shifted her weight to one booted foot. "I'd have fumbled and stumbled my way through it, one way or another."

He didn't doubt it. Cindy had a lot of gumption.

But Blake wasn't sure what he could do to help, other than encourage her to buy some dresses. Maybe fix her hair differently. That would be a good start.

Cindy had never been what you'd call pretty. But that was because she didn't do anything to help her looks. She didn't use makeup, perfume or body lotions. And as far as he knew, she'd never worn anything other than denim and flannel.

The small-town tomboy was definitely going to have to change her style.

Of course, it wasn't as though Blake knew how to coach a woman through that sort of thing. But Cindy was a special friend who was like a kid sister to him. And catching Robby's eye obviously meant a lot to her.

He tossed her a sympathetic grin. "You're going to need a makeover, Sprout."

She brightened. "So, you'll help me?"

"Sure." He'd give it a try—if he could. And if she'd let him have a free hand.

She smiled at him, with glistening eyes that were the color of new-mowed hay. He hadn't noticed before, but they were actually pretty. And far more expressive than he'd remembered.

When she blinked, he realized her long, spiky black lashes curled naturally. Hey, that was a plus. She wouldn't need to use any of that black goop women brushed on them.

He looked at her hair. She always plaited her long curly red mop in a single braid that hung down her back or in that slick granny-type topknot she was wearing now. On some women, the style looked sexy when they let wispy strands hang free and loose.

He began to pull out the pins that held her hair in place. If she was going to wear it up, she needed to fix it differently.

Her eyes widened and her lips parted. "What are you doing?"

"Seeing what this looks like down."

She touched the side of her hair with a dirty hand. "Now it's a mess."

He had to agree, as he used his fingers to comb out the clumps of curls. But as the sun lit upon golden highlights, his hand slowed.

Wow. He hadn't realized how thick, how rich...how shiny her hair was.

He dropped his hands to his sides. God knows he couldn't coach her on how to style a new hairdo. "Our first stop will be at the Cut N Curl."

"Oh, no," she said, taking a step back. "Not there. Grandpa took me once or twice when I was a kid, and they tugged and pulled on my hair something awful. After that, I refused to go and have been trimming it myself for years."

No one needed to tell Blake how stubborn Cindy could be when she set her mind to something or dug in her heels.

So he played her game. "If you're all fired up for a makeover, you're going to have to do something different with it. And God knows I can't coach you on how to come up with a new hairstyle."

She tugged at one of the wavy strands, pulling it taut. "You think someone there can actually get this bush to obey a comb and brush?"

"Sure." He offered her a smile. "We can talk about it more in the house. Just let me put Cutter into the corral so he can stretch out his legs."

"Mind if I help?" she asked.

"Not at all. It'll be nice to have your company. I've missed you, Sprout."

And he had.

She'd been a pest when he'd first come to

live here. But a sweet pest who'd actually grown on him. And now, eight years after he'd moved away from the ranch, it was his job to help her attract the attention of Robby Bradshaw, a guy who'd better treat her right, or he'd have a fight on his hands.

Blake wouldn't stand by and let anyone hurt the young woman he cared about.

As he led Cutter to the corral, he watched as Cindy strode ahead to unlatch the gate. He couldn't help noticing the natural sway to her gait, the nice curve of her hips.

Years ago, she'd been all knees and elbows.

But she'd sure grown into those jeans.

Dinner at the Tumbling T Ranch was the usual, no-fuss, no-muss fare. Ever since the old cowboy's wife had passed on and kitchen duty had fallen on Tuck, he fixed easy meals that required very little time at the stove.

Tuck couldn't cook a lick, but he was a whiz with a can opener, lunch meat and two slabs of bread.

"Can I get you some more beans?" Tuck asked.

"Nope. One helping is plenty for me." As a teenager, Blake had gotten pretty sick of canned food, especially pork and beans, which had to be Tuck's all-time favorite filler.

"How about you, Cindy Lou?" The gray-haired man lifted the pan from the stove, as though willing to carry it to the kitchen table and serve her.

"No, thanks, Grandpa. That bologna sandwich filled me up."

After spooning a hefty third helping into his bowl, Tuck returned to the scarred oak table and took his seat. "It sure is good to have you home, boy."

Blake grinned, his chest swelling just from sitting at the familiar kitchen table and knowing he was welcome anytime. "It's nice being back."

As a teenager, he'd been sent to live on the Tumbling T because his grandfather, who'd been Tuck's old army buddy, had hoped the tough-as-leather cowboy could give Blake some direction. And after butting heads with Blake more than a time or two, Tuck had done just that.

"So what's the latest town gossip?" Blake asked, knowing there was always something going on in nearby Blossom.

"Just the ruckus that's brewing between the

fair board and the Committee for Moral Behavior."

"The Committee for Moral Behavior?" he asked. "What's that?"

"A group of fussbudgets who don't think people should have any fun," Tuck said, digging into his bowl of beans. When he looked up, spoon held high and overflowing, he added, "But no one is going to tell me when and where I can drink. Or what I can spend my money on."

"What have they got against the fair board?" Blake asked.

Tuck had his mouth full, so Cindy explained. "Two years ago, at the county fair, a gypsy fortune-teller told some of the townspeople they would strike it rich. Then, when a slick-talking shyster came to town, selling stock in a real-estate venture, a lot of folks blindly jumped in and lost more than their shirts in the phony land deal. So blaming the carnies as a bad element, the fair board decided not to allow the carnival people to set up their rides and games along the midway last year. Needless to say, attendance was way down."

"And the fair was a complete bust," Tuck added.

Blake imagined it would be. People from

all the neighboring dry counties had flocked to the fair in the past, and not just because Blossom County was wet and the beer garden had been a big draw. The kids had a ton of fun at the carnival and along the midway. And they'd dragged their parents to the fair time and again.

"The county coffers are still suffering," Cindy added.

"Aw heck," Tuck said with a frown. "The fuss has gotten so big and out of hand that a body can't step foot into Blossom without listening to the squabble. Everyone has been taking sides, and I swear a brawl is going to break out one of these days."

Blake thought people ought to be held accountable for their own foolish business ventures. "What kind of nut would listen to the advice of a fortune-teller they met at a carnival?"

"Some folks don't have the sense of a turkey gobbler," Tuck said, as he scooted his chair away from the table, rubbed his belly and stood. "Well, I'm going to walk off my dinner, while I have a chat with Mary Ellen."

Blake and Cindy watched the old man head for the service porch, take his hat from the peg by the door and go outside, Shep trotting along after him.

Cindy tore at the edge of the paper towel she'd used as a napkin and studied the closed back door. "It always makes me feel kind of sad when he does that. He sure must have loved my grandma something fierce."

Blake nodded. The old man probably did miss his wife. But as a teenager, Blake had followed Tuck enough times to believe his real reason for the after-dinner walk was because the canned beans he consumed at all three meals played havoc with his digestive system.

But other than a crooked grin, Blake kept his thoughts to himself.

"Hey." Cindy elbowed him. "Let's put the dishes in the sink and let them soak while we have a bowl of rocky road ice cream."

"Sure." Blake never could turn down dessert, especially anything chocolate.

A few minutes later, they carried their bowls and spoons out to the back porch, where they took a seat and enjoyed the night sounds of crickets chirping and bullfrogs croaking down by the creek. Cutter nickered in the corral.

"It's pretty tonight," Cindy said as she studied the new moon that rested in a star-studded sky.

"It sure is. I've missed the Tumbling T. It's great to be home."

That was nice to know. Cindy liked the fact

that Blake still considered the ranch his home, because the truth was, even if she couldn't have him in a romantic sense, she appreciated his friendship. And right now, she looked forward to his expertise and getting his sage advice.

Shoot, who else could coach her about romance? After all, he'd had more experience than men twice his age. At least, that's what she'd always suspected.

He'd had his pick of any of the girls at Sam Houston High. And from what she'd overheard, there'd been quite a few young ladies who'd been blessed with his kisses, if not a whole lot more.

Cindy had always felt a stab of envy when she thought about the girls he'd dated back then. But that was because she hadn't had to do anything more than look in the mirror or check inside her bra to see that she couldn't compete—at least not *that* way—with any of them. And even though she filled her bra a little better these days, she still couldn't compete with the cutesy women, many of whom still wore their blouses too small and their pants too tight.

But all that was going to change, thanks to a new attitude and a tutor.

Blake took a big spoonful of rocky road, obviously enjoying the taste. Then he slid her a probing look. "What's so special about Robby Bradshaw?"

Not a whole lot, she supposed. He was kind of sweet. And smart as all get-out. Of course, he was also the first guy who'd ever shown her any attention. Well, he was the first one whose attention actually interested her.

"It's kind of hard to explain," she said.

"Try me."

She thought for a moment, choosing her words. The fact was, until she and Robby actually got a chance to sit and talk, there wasn't a whole lot she knew about him, other than he was nice and had always treated her with respect—and not just because she could outride or outrope him. "Robby is a business major, with a minor in accounting."

"And that's his only appeal? Are you after him for the money he might make?"

"No," she snapped. "I never said I wanted to marry him. I just want to date him. And as far as I'm concerned, the fact that he's making something out of himself is a good thing."

"Yeah. I guess so. But I don't want you to settle for the first guy who comes along."

She blew out a sigh. "I'm not settling."

Of course, she wasn't at all sure she was

telling the truth. But she was ready to change the focus of their conversation. "So what about you? Surely there has to be a special lady in your life."

He shrugged. "I don't know about that. Plenty of women chase after me—one in particular—but I'm not ready to get hitched. Not now. And maybe not ever."

That didn't surprise her. He'd always had his pick of women. Why should he settle for just one?

She wondered about the gals who chased after him now. They had to be gorgeous, no doubt, with breasts that bulged out of tiny lace bras, bare midriffs, short skirts and swivel-hipped walks. Women who'd breeze right past Cindy without even seeing her, she suspected.

The girls he'd dated in high school had never given Cindy a howdy-do back then and still didn't give her much more than that whenever she ran into them in town.

But maybe, if Blake helped her with a make-over, they'd be friendlier and see her as an equal.

But women weren't her main concern.

"I wish men found me more appealing," she admitted.

Of course, Blake was the one man she'd most like to have fall for her. But only a fool would bother drooling over the impossible, while the possible sat ready for the taking.

Blake reached for her hand and gave it a squeeze. "Listen to me, Sprout. You've got a heart as big as Texas, and you're loyal, too. A man would be lucky to have you in his life."

Deep in her Lone Star heart, she knew that. But getting a man to take that first look? Now that was the problem.

He ran his knuckles along her cheek, causing her heart to thump and jump and do all kinds of crazy things. "I mean that, honey."

"Thanks." A lump formed in her throat, and she had to blink back the tears. Darn him for being so sweet.

"So tell me more about Robby."

Huh? How had Robby sidled into the conversation? "What about him?"

"For starters, what does he look like?"

She shrugged. He was about the same height as Blake—just under six feet. But he wasn't nearly as solid. And he was pretty fair-complexioned. Of course, that was to be expected. Robby probably had to study day and night. When would he get a chance to go outdoors in the sunshine or work out?

"I guess he's kind of cute," she said.

"You guess?"

She blew out a sigh. "He's got blond hair and brown eyes. A nice smile."

"Is he good to you?"

"Well, darn it, Blake. How the heck am I supposed to know that? He's so shy we've barely even talked."

"I'm not trying to give you a hard time."

She knew he wasn't. But it just didn't feel right talking about Robby in front of Blake. Not when simply sitting next to the good-looking cowboy made her want to compare the two.

And poor Robby couldn't hold a candle to Blake.

Nope. It wasn't right. If anyone understood how unfair comparisons felt, it was Cindy.

"I'll tell you what," he said. "We'll go into town tomorrow and stop at the Cut N Curl and the Mercantile. And before the sun sets, you'll be a new woman."

Blake made it sound so easy, and she hoped he was right.

Cindy wasn't sure when it began to matter what men thought of her, but she suspected it had started long before she'd spotted Robby fishing at the lake.

Either way, she was ready for some changes in her life. And tomorrow wasn't going to be a day too soon.

Chapter Two

"You know, I've missed those guys."

Cindy glanced at the handsome cowboy at her side, then followed his gaze to the front of the courthouse, where Dutch and Buster sat. The two crusty old men spent the daylight hours parked on that green-wood-and-wrought-iron bench and watched the world go by.

"You never used to like this town," she said. "Or too many of the residents."

"It's funny what a few years' perspective will give a man. Dutch and Buster are a hoot. Haven't you ever taken time to talk to them?"

Dutch, the tall, lanky one of the two, chose

that very moment to spit a stream of tobacco into the rusted coffee can that sat on the sidewalk and served as a joint spittoon.

His aim wasn't very good, and Cindy could have sworn he hit Buster's boot.

"I've never really chatted with them, although Grandpa does. They seem kind of crotchety, if you ask me."

"Only if they don't like you." Blake chuckled. "Those two don't miss much. And they've got an interesting philosophy of life, especially when it comes to the people who live in Blossom."

Cindy had her own opinion about some of the townspeople, too. And she wondered if that came from sitting on the outside looking in, much like the two old men did.

"Come on," Blake said. "I want to say hello to them."

As she and Blake approached, Dutch remained seated while Buster stood.

The short, heavyset man wore a stained white shirt, green suspenders, a dusty red baseball cap and a smile. He reached out a gnarly hand to Blake. "Well, now. Aren't you a sight for sore eyes."

Blake accepted Buster's shake, then reached

out to Dutch. "It's good to see you guys. Looks like you're just as ornery as ever."

"And we're gonna get a whole lot ornerier," Dutch said as he leaned forward in his seat to spit into the can. "That dad-burn bunch of moral misfits aim to run us off our bench."

Buster crossed his arms over a belly that put a real strain on his suspenders. "But they'll have a fight on their hands. Nobody's going to tell us where we can sit. Or where we can spit."

Dutch leaned back in the bench and stretched out his long legs. "A couple of revenuers tried to run my daddy off the farm once. And they got a load of buckshot in the side of that fancy black car they drove."

Buster took his seat beside his longtime friend. "This is a public bench. And just because we've got a little silver in our hair and gold in our teeth doesn't mean we got metal in our brains. We're not going to let those uppity moral morons tell us what to do."

"By the way," Dutch said to Blake. "I wanna congratulate you. Heard you went eight seconds with ol' Flame Thrower. Ain't no one done that, yet."

Blake smiled. "It was a good day. And a good ride."

"Folks are talking about the Blossom

County rodeo and how happy they are that you're going to compete. Why, Buster and I might even leave our bench and come watch."

"I hope you do."

"How's Tuck doing?" Buster asked Cindy. "We heard he was down at the clinic last week."

Cindy's heart nearly jumped out of her chest. She didn't know anything about her grandfather's visit to the doctor. "He doesn't appear to be sick."

"Well, it ain't nothin' a little romancin' won't cure," Dutch said with a chuckle. "We heard there's a pretty nurse who works there. We been meanin' to go have us a look-see ourselves."

Grandpa was interested in a woman? She supposed that was better than him having medical problems and needing to see the doctor. But Cindy couldn't imagine the old cowboy having a romantic streak. He was still pining over the loss of his wife. Dutch and Buster must be mistaken.

"I hate to run," Blake told the men, "but it's burning daylight and we still have a few errands to run. I hope to see you both at the rodeo."

"We'll be there," Buster said.

Blake nudged Cindy. "We've got work to do, unless you've changed your mind."

"I haven't." She picked up her pace to match his, as they cut across the lawn toward the shops that lined the north side of the town square. "You know, Dutch and Buster were right. Everyone in town is happy you're back."

"Only because I've made a name for myself. You know as well as I do that wasn't always the case."

Blake was right. When he first came to Blossom, people had looked down on him. He'd always said it was because he was half Indian. But Cindy and Grandpa had suspected his initial don't-mess-with-me attitude had played a part.

"I don't have any ties to Blossom," he said, "other than you and Tuck. And I'm only riding in the rodeo because Jason and Trace asked me to."

Mayor Jason Strong and Sheriff Trace McCabe had become friends of Blake's back in high school, after they'd stepped in during a teenage brawl and saved Blake from getting the tar beaten out of him.

Blake's loyalty to the two men was admirable, and she respected him for it. His loyalty to her and Grandpa was admirable, too.

But she really had to get her mind back on the business at hand.

"Where are we going first?" she asked.

"To the Mercantile." He placed a hand on her shoulder, guiding her toward the upscale dress shop.

Cindy purchased her clothing at Family Fashions, a discount store that made shopping a handy, one-stop experience for her and Grandpa. And the last winter, when she'd acquired what seemed like a sudden interest in women's fashion, she'd made a point of walking by the Mercantile whenever she was in town.

She liked to peer through the big picture window at the mannequins on display. But even though she was often tempted to step inside, she never had. She would feel a bit awkward entering a fancy place like that by herself.

So having Blake as her guide was going to be an adventure, for more reasons than one.

When they reached the entrance, he dropped his hand, leaving her feeling almost abandoned, as he opened the door to let her in.

A burst of nervousness buzzed through her as they walked into the shop filled with racks of stylish outfits. And although she wanted to slip her hand in his, she resisted the urge.

After all, she'd been the one who'd agreed to a makeover. And the one who'd decided to set her sights on Robby and ask for Blake's help. So she'd have to be woman enough to face her nerves head-on.

"May I help you?" a well-dressed saleslady asked.

"I'd like to buy a couple of outfits for my friend," Blake told her.

Cindy nudged him with her elbow. "I only asked for your advice. You're not paying for anything." She patted the small purse she carried. "Besides, I have plenty of cash saved up for this."

"Well, you can put your money away. I'm paying for everything." Blake looked at the saleslady. "We'd like something young and stylish. Can you give us some suggestions?"

"Of course." The salesclerk indicated a chair where Blake could wait. Then she eyed Cindy carefully. "Let's get you in the fitting room, and I'll see what I can do."

Twenty minutes later, Blake continued to sit on a red-velvet-covered settee that was so delicate he hoped it would hold him. His black Stetson rested on the cushion beside him as he thumbed through a fashion magazine.

He knew the Mercantile was a women's dress shop, but you'd think they'd set out reading material that might interest a man who had to tag along. Of course, he hadn't been inside a place like this for years, not since his mother had dragged him to the mall back home and made him wait while she tried on every darn thing in several stores. He didn't like shopping with a woman back then, and he sure as heck didn't like it now.

But this was a favor for Cindy.

"Are you ready for a fashion show?" the brunette saleslady asked with what he suspected was an I-work-on-commission smile.

"Sure." He set down the magazine and stretched out his legs. They may as well get the show on the road. Then they could get out of here.

"The first number is a sundress designed by Catarini, a new designer out of New York."

Oh, for Pete's sake. The woman could can the commentary. All he cared about was whether it looked good on Cindy and whether she liked it.

But as Cindy walked timidly from the fitting room, wearing a slinky green sundress that showed off a heck of a lot more of her than the jeans and shirt she'd worn in there, he nearly dropped his teeth.

The petite redhead tugged at the material that slid tauntingly over her hips. "What do you think? Is it too small?"

No. Yes. Heck, he didn't know.

She turned around and glanced over her shoulder to get a different view of her reflection. "I'm not comfortable with my legs showing."

He didn't know why. She had great legs. Not very long, of course, since she only stood a whisper over five feet. But they were shaped perfectly.

"The dress looks good," he said, his voice coming out in a choked whisper. *Real good.*

"Do you think Robby will pay more attention to me if I wear something like this?" she asked.

Heck, yeah. Unless the bookworm was blind. All Blake knew was that it would sure make him sit up and take notice.

She tugged at the hem, which rested just above the knee, apparently still stressing about the length.

"Why aren't you comfortable with your legs showing?" he asked.

"Someone once told me that my knees were

knobby, so I've kept them covered up ever since." She glanced in the mirror, checking her hemline. Then she looked at him as though wanting confirmation.

Something told him that he might have been the one who had teased her. "If it was me, I'm sorry. You have great legs and knees. I was either lying, or you outgrew that coltish stage." Then he looked at the salesclerk. "We'll take it."

The woman clapped her hands without making much of a sound. "I knew you'd like it. She has a lovely shape and can wear those form-fitting outfits."

"I'm a little self-conscious dressed like this," Cindy admitted.

"You shouldn't be, dear." The woman grinned. "Now go in and try on those black cropped pants and the top that goes with it."

Before long, Cindy returned wearing a pair of pants that rode low on her hips and a jungle-print blouse that left a strip of her waistline bare. Blake knew that was the style. And he liked the look, especially on other women. But he wasn't sure he wanted Cindy parading the streets of Blossom like that.

He'd had no idea what she'd been hiding behind denim and flannel.

Ten minutes later, Blake paid for the purchases, which included three different pants outfits, two dresses—one yellow, the other black—and a pair of black heels. The sales-clerk also rang up the white silky blouse, blue skirt and strappy sandals Cindy was wearing.

As the saleslady carefully packed each item in a piece of tissue, she smiled.

No doubt about it. That *had* to be an I'm-counting-my-hefty-commission grin. But what the heck. Cindy deserved a shopping spree, and he was happy he could provide her one.

"You don't mind if I wear this out, do you?" Cindy glanced at the skirt she wore, again tug-ging at the hem even though it really wasn't too short. "It's kind of skimpy."

"And very fashionable," the clerk added. "You look fabulous."

Blake had to agree. But he still wasn't sure he wanted her walking around town like that. And he didn't have the foggiest notion why.

Just looking out for her, he supposed. That's all.

As they headed for the door, he studied the young woman who walked in front of him.

The stretchy blue fabric caressed the curves she'd been hiding beneath baggy denim, and he doubted there was a man alive who wouldn't take a second look. At least from the neck down.

If she learned to fix her hair and put on some makeup, she'd actually be able to set her sights on someone a lot better than Robby Bradshaw—an assessment Blake easily made without even meeting the guy.

As they stepped out into the late-afternoon sun, Cindy balked. "I feel half-dressed, no matter what that saleslady told me. Maybe I ought to run back inside and put on my jeans."

"Don't bother. You may as well get used to the attention. Those new clothes look nice on you. That saleslady wasn't just stringing you along."

Cindy beamed, then threw her arms around him and gave him a quick hug. "Thank you."

"You're welcome." As he returned her embrace, his hands slid along the sleek fabric of a blouse that rode a little too high up her back, and a jolt of heat shimmied through his blood. He dropped his arms and stepped back.

Cindy may have been twenty-two, but to him she was just a kid. A babe in the woods.

A woman-child poised on the verge of consenting adulthood. And he meant to look after her until she could handle being at that stage in her life.

"Come on. Next stop is the Cut N Curl."

* * *

A bell over the door announced their arrival, as Blake and Cindy entered the only beauty shop in town, a busy place with a bright orange-and-yellow decor. The scent of hairspray and nail polish lingered in the warm and stuffy room.

It looked different than it had the last time Cindy had been in here.

A petite woman with big hair the color of an orange neon light sat behind the appointment desk. She looked up and flashed them a cheerful smile. "Hello, there. Welcome to the Cut N Curl. My name is Wanda Mae. How can I help you?"

Cindy looked at Blake. He seemed to know what he was doing, or at least what he had in mind, so she let him do the talking.

"Does someone have time for a cut and style?" he asked.

"I'm sure we can fit it in." Wanda Mae scanned her appointment book.

Cindy took that time to survey the busy room. Each of the customers had a personal beauty expert working over her, except for the lady with her gray hair rolled in pink curlers, who waited alone under the hood of a big yellow dryer, and the gal with her hair covered in little foil squares, who thumbed through a gossip magazine.

A matronly woman appeared to be dozing while her bare feet soaked in a bubbling tub of water. Getting a pedicure, Cindy supposed.

One young girl, who looked as though her hair had been dyed with jet-black ink, sat before a mirror, watching closely as a tall blonde beautician took a scissors to locks that were already short and scraggly.

The place was amazing, and not at all what Cindy had remembered. She couldn't believe the lengths women went to improve their looks.

Had that been her problem in the past? Too little fuss and effort?

Wanda Mae clicked her tongue and furrowed her brow, as she twisted a lock of neon-orange hair and studied the book. "We're a little full, but I suppose I could do it myself."

Oh, no. Cindy could imagine herself walking out of here with her hair the same color as a highway worker's safety vest.

She tugged at Blake's chambray shirtsleeve and cupped her mouth to indicate a secret. As he bent toward her, she whispered, "If she so much as starts toward me with a bottle of hair dye, I'm going to poke her in the nose and knock her on her fanny."

Blake peered over the reception desk and looked at the appointment book.

"Maybe someone has time to give her a manicure or pedicure," he suggested. "Then you can fit her in when one of the hairstylists has time."

"Now, that I can do," Wanda Mae said with a smile. "We'll give her the works."

"Sounds good to me." Blake reached for the doorknob. "What time should I come back?"

"Give us until five o'clock. We'll have her as pretty as a picture."

As Cindy watched Blake saunter out of the beauty salon on his own, she had half a notion to follow him. What had she gotten herself into?

"It'll be just a few minutes," Wanda Mae said with a flashy smile. "The manicurist will be ready for you as soon as she finishes polishing that lady's toes. And while you're waiting, you can enter our baby pool."

Cindy was almost afraid to ask. She'd heard of baby showers. "What's a baby pool?"

"Tammy Wright, one of the gals who lives in Blossom, is due to have a baby at the end of August. Rumor has it that the doctor says the little one is a boy, but don't tell anyone I told you."

Cindy knew Tammy; they'd gone to school together. And even though they'd never socialized much other than at school, Tammy had been one of the few girls she'd considered a friend.

Wanda Mae whipped out a poster board that listed names, dates and hours. "It only costs two dollars to get in the pool. All you have to do is pick a day and a block of time that hasn't been chosen. Then write down whether you think it's a boy or girl. The winner gets two hundred dollars."

Oh, why not? Cindy dug through her purse and handed Wanda Mae two one-dollar bills. Then she chose August twenty-eight. She'd heard most babies came in the middle of the night, so she took the hours between midnight and six in the morning. And since Wanda Mae had mentioned that the doctor said it was a boy, she figured it would be silly to guess Tammy's baby would be a girl.

After returning the chart to Wanda Mae, she took a seat near the front window. She didn't have to wait long until she was called.

From that moment on, Cindy was pampered and fussed over until she thought she could really get used to the special attention.

She couldn't help marveling at how soft her

hands were. She could have sworn they were going to stay permanently chapped. Her skin smelled good, too. Like orange blossoms and cream.

And her toes sported a pretty pink polish that matched her fingernails.

She'd even agreed to have her eyebrows waxed. Ouch.

As she sat in a swivel chair before a big gold mirror, she could hardly recognize the image of the woman who looked back at her.

The beautician studied the awkward strands, tugging, poking. "It's a beautiful color. You really ought to wear it down and show it off."

"I've always had a hard time running a comb through it," Cindy explained. "And if I don't bind it up somehow, by nighttime it looks like I barely survived a Texas twister."

"We'll see what a little styling and conditioning does about that."

Moments later, the woman got to work, and Cindy sat back and watched.

After a conditioning process and a practically tangle-free comb out, Cindy decided she would have to stock up on some conditioner to use at home. Then she watched the beautician go to work, combing, lifting, snipping. And before long, the woman took a rounded brush and a blow dryer, carefully styling as the hair dried.

"Well," the stylist said, after shutting off the hot air and handing Cindy a handheld mirror. "What do you think?"

She didn't know what to think, other than that the results were magical. She had no idea how long it would last, but it looked pretty darn good, even if she did say so herself. "I'd always considered my hair one of my biggest flaws. And I can't believe what you've done to it."

"Thanks. I take pride in my job, especially when I have something to work with. You're a pretty woman. Now all you need is a dab of lipstick. Why don't you get it out of your purse."

"I...don't wear makeup," Cindy said.

"Well, I suppose you don't really need it. But we've got some new products on display that a lot of our clients have been raving about." She hollered to the front of the shop. "Wanda Mae, will you bring me a tube of Pretty in Pink?"

By the time the women had finished with her, Cindy held a sack full of beauty supplies and a detailed list of instructions for their use. And even though she still felt like a guppy in a mason jar, her self-esteem had sure gotten a shot in the arm.

But that was nothing compared to the jolt she received when Blake strode into the Cut N Curl at five o'clock.

As Blake's eyes lit on Cindy, he froze in his tracks.

Talk about beauty makeovers. She'd gone from Calamity Jane to a redheaded Cinderella in a few short hours.

"What do you think?" she asked, nibbling on her bottom lip.

Heck, he didn't know what to think.

Her hair hung loose to her shoulders in a sexy array of curls that seemed to dance whenever she moved her head. He wasn't sure what they'd done to her eyebrows, but they sure made a guy focus on those expressive green eyes.

And the pink lipstick she wore made her lips look…well, they looked just plain kissable.

"Is it too much?" she asked.

No. It was just right. But he couldn't seem to open his mouth to tell her.

"For Pete's sake, Blake, you're making me so darn nervous I could bust."

"You look fine. Nice." He had to force the words out, as well as make himself breathe.

He'd expected a makeover to help her look somewhat attractive. But he hadn't expected her to bubble over with…whatever it was that was bursting from the seams of that little blue skirt and white silky blouse.

"Don't let him kid you," Wanda Mae said. "I saw the way he nearly tripped over his jaw when he took one look at you. My gosh, girl, you're as pretty as a fashion model."

"Do you think Robby will be surprised?" Cindy asked him.

Flabbergasted would be more like it.

Suddenly, a flood of responsibility washed over Blake. He couldn't just let Cindy out on the streets looking like that. Not without some way of protecting her from a pack of males on the prowl. It would be like throwing a calf to the coyotes. "You're not going out in public like that."

"What do you mean?"

"At least, not without me. Not yet. You're not ready for Robby, or any other guy, for that matter."

She slapped her hands on her hips, and the familiar sass erupted in her eyes. "I've taken a lot of guff over the years from some of the kids I've gone to school with, but I'm not about to let you tease me, too."

"Tease you?" God knows he'd done his share of ribbing her in the past about one thing or another, but he wasn't teasing about her looks. Or the appeal she was bound to have on the unsuspecting single males in Blossom. And some of the married ones, too, he suspected.

She slid him a pout that actually made her look all the more sexy. "I don't need you to rub in the fact that I haven't had any real dates."

"You've never had a date?" Wanda Mae laughed. "Well, that's about to change. Maybe I'd better go into the back room and find a stick that you can use to chase off the men whenever you come into town."

The flashy orange-haired woman was right.

Blake took Cindy by the hand. "Listen, honey. I told you I'd coach you. And that's what I intend to do. You look great. And there isn't a man alive who wouldn't agree with me. But men are a strange breed, and I just want to make sure you can hold your own."

"Listen here, Blake Gray Feather. I have no problem holding my own with men. Never had, never will."

"I'm not talking about riding and roping, Cindy."

"Knock it off. I quit competing with boys in high school."

He rolled his eyes and blew out a ragged sigh. "Some guys aren't honest. And they have ulterior motives."

"I might be inexperienced, but I read books and magazines. And I watch TV. So you don't have to worry about me."

She talked a good story, but he had his doubts. Some men would take advantage of her innocence. And that was something Blake couldn't allow to happen.

"I'm only going to be in town for another couple weeks, then you'll be on your own. And I want to leave knowing you won't let some fast-talking, womanizing cowboy sweep you off your feet." His gaze dropped down to her toes, which had been newly polished.

Oh, for Pete's sake. She even had beautiful feet.

Blake blew out a ragged sigh.

What in the world had he created?

And worse, what had he gotten himself into?

Chapter Three

As they carried their packages to the pickup, Blake didn't say much to Cindy. He figured she was still trying to get used to the change in her appearance.

And so was he.

He'd known she would benefit from a make-over. But he hadn't been prepared for the actual difference a new outfit and hairstyle would make.

How had he ever missed seeing her potential?

"Thank you for the new clothes and all the beauty treatments," she said. "I really should have paid for it myself."

"I wanted to do it. Besides, it was a way for me to repay you and your grandfather for putting up with me when I was a mouthy teen."

"You weren't so bad," she said.

"Not even that first day when I teased you about the color of your hair?"

The day Blake had arrived on the ranch, he'd tugged on one of her braids and called her Carrot Top. She'd merely glared at him until he looked away. Then she'd lowered her head and rushed him like a billy goat with its tail on fire.

"When I picked myself up off the floor, you slapped your hands on your hips, glared down and said, 'Carrot tops are green, city boy.'"

She smiled. "You got the point. And you only called me Carrot Top once."

Yeah, but from that day on, he'd started calling her Sprout instead. "If I hadn't been off balance, I would have stayed on my feet."

Cindy grinned, green eyes glimmering with the memory of his reaction to her sneak attack. "I'll never forget that wide-eyed gape on your face when I stood over you."

"You had a lot more spunk as a kid than I gave you credit for."

"I still do."

She certainly did. There'd always been a lot

more to Cindy Tucker than met the eye. And what met the eye now was a pleasant surprise.

"I'm glad you came to live with us," she admitted, "even though I resented the attention Grandpa gave to you."

"That's something I understand now. You'd had Tuck to yourself for years, and I required a lot of his time and attention."

She elbowed him gently. "But it all worked out. We sort of became a family."

They had, he supposed. Cindy and Tuck had offered Blake something he'd never had before, even though he'd never completely fit in.

Of course, he'd never fit into his real family, either. In some ways, he supposed, he was too much like his Indian father. Different. An outsider.

At least that's the conclusion he'd come to after growing up and gaining an adult perspective.

But he really only favored his father in looks. Unlike Blake, Clint Gray Feather had been a liar and a womanizer who'd broken his fair-haired wife's heart time and again. She'd finally gotten smart, filed for divorce and moved out of state. But not before losing faith in men and finding happiness in a bottle.

Now that he was older and wiser, Blake

suspected that every time his mom looked at her half-Indian son, especially when she'd been drinking, she'd been reminded of the man who'd lied and cheated. As a result, their mother-son relationship had suffered.

Things were better between them now, he supposed. Although not a lot. He'd learned to live with the kind of relationship he and his mom did have.

And he'd learned to live with being different and not fitting in, except in the rodeo world.

He took the packages from Cindy, slid them behind the driver's door, then set the alarm on his truck. A lot of people never locked their doors in Blossom, but Blake had grown up in the inner city of Los Angeles. It was hard to shake his skepticism and his belief that there were people out there who'd rob a man blind if he'd let them.

As Cindy began to circle the Chevy pickup to climb into the passenger side, he stopped her. "I'm hungry. And unless you've learned to cook over the past few years, we won't get anything other than beans or canned spaghetti at the ranch. Let's eat out. We can call Tuck and tell him we'll bring something home to him."

"All right."

The last time Blake had been in town, he'd

had a great meal at the Bee Hive Diner. He could still remember thinking they served the best chicken-fried steak he'd ever eaten, complete with creamy, home-style mashed potatoes smothered in gravy.

He placed a hand on Cindy's shoulder. "Come on."

His palm lingered on the soft fabric of her blouse, as his fingers grazed the skin along her upper back. It took him a moment to realize what he was doing, to sense the possessive way he touched her. And when he did, he quickly dropped his arm to his side.

For Pete's sake, she was practically family.

Still, each time he stole a glance at her, each time he looked into those springtime-green eyes or noticed those womanly curves, he found himself forgetting that he was supposed to be looking out for her.

Maybe he ought to suggest she wear denim and flannel whenever he was around.

As they neared the courthouse, Buster stood up from his seat on the bench and let out a long, appreciative wolf whistle.

Cindy giggled. "If he weren't such a crusty old man, I'd be flattered."

"Buster might be pushing eighty, but he's still able to appreciate a pretty lady. So go ahead and enjoy the flattery." Blake led her along the walkway, past Strong Bank and back to the south end of town square.

The Bee Hive still had the same sign out front. The same yellow-checkered café-style curtains that covered the bottom half of the windows. He just hoped they had the same owners, or at least the same cook.

As they entered, Blake made a quick scan of the diner. Things didn't appear to have changed. They had the same brown Formica tables, yellow vinyl seats and corner booths.

A beehive mural, complete with a swarm of honeybees had been painted on the wall since Blake had last eaten here. But that was about all that seemed different.

The aroma of a down-home meal and the yeasty smell of fresh-baked dinner rolls wafted through the diner, taunting his hunger and making his stomach sit up and beg.

A fifty-something woman with her gray-streaked hair swept into a bouffant twist, grabbed a couple of menus. "Two for dinner?"

"Yes." Blake placed a hand on Cindy's back, allowing her to go first.

She didn't get more than three steps across the floor, when her foot slipped and her arms flew up. He caught her before she could hit the ground.

Her citrus scent accosted him as the silky soft strands of her hair brushed softly against his cheek. The feel of the petite, womanly body in his arms chased aside the platonic affection he'd always felt for the country tomboy, which ought to have scared the spit right out of him. But for some crazy reason, he held her close, afraid to let go.

And afraid not to.

She turned her head and caught his eye. For a stunning couple of heartbeats, their gazes locked as something passed between them, something pulse-spinning and almost surreal.

But Blake shook it off. "Are you all right?"

She nodded. "I...think so. These darn new shoes..."

"I'm so sorry," the hostess said. "We just had these floors polished. Maybe we should put up a warning sign."

Blake helped Cindy to her feet, wondering if he ought to help her adjust the hem of her skirt to make sure she hadn't given the kitchen staff a view of her panties.

He didn't, of course. But he continued to hold on to her arm, his hand on her back—just making sure neither the floor nor her brand-new soles gave her any more trouble, he told himself.

"I'm okay," she said. "Just a little embarrassed."

"At least we're the only ones here," he told her. "The dinner crowd has yet to trickle in, so it'll be our secret."

She tossed him a bright-eyed smile, one that only vaguely resembled the grins she used to flash him when they were younger, when they'd shared other secrets.

He glanced down at the strappy white sandals, at the bright pink polish on her pretty toes. "You're going to have to practice wearing those things at home before you go out with Robby."

"And I'll have to remember to stay off slick floors," she added. The flush on her cheeks merely made her prettier.

Robby was in for a heady surprise—a thought that didn't sit very well. Maybe because Blake didn't know the guy Cindy had set her sights on. Didn't know whether he'd approve of him or not.

The hostess led them to a corner booth and placed two menus on the table.

Cindy slid in first, her legs squeaking against the vinyl seat as she scooted to the inside, which made him wonder if her hem needed another adjustment.

He swore under his breath.

So what if her skirt wasn't covering her right? What business was it of his?

He took a seat across from her, and before long the Bee Hive began to fill with people.

They'd no more than placed their orders when two older kids at a nearby table began to talk about the upcoming county fair.

"The fair was a joke last year," the preteen boy said. "Who wants to look at a bunch of prize livestock or wander through those dumb flower shows?"

"Not me," replied the girl who appeared to be his older sister. "Without a carnival, there's no reason to even go."

"Tommy's neighbor is on the fair board," the boy said. "And he was told that they're probably going to let the carnival people come back this year."

"I sure hope so," the girl replied. "It was boring without any rides or games."

The woman who sat at their table—their mother, Blake assumed—took a sip of coffee before joining the conversation. "The carnival issue hasn't been decided yet. A lot of people believe the carnies are a bad element and shouldn't be allowed into town. And your father and I agree."

Blake returned his attention to his dinner companion. "I see the lines have been drawn on the fair debate. Have you taken sides?"

"I've always loved the carnival. Last year's fair was a huge disappointment, as far as I'm concerned. How about you?"

Blake shrugged. "It's not anything I'm going to even think about. I'll be out of here before the fair's opening day."

Yet the fact was, he didn't like some of the comments he'd overheard while he wandered through town, waiting for Cindy to get her hair done. When he'd heard the "them versus us" arguments, he'd sympathized with the carnies, outsiders like himself.

But he kept his mouth shut, not about to reveal his Achilles' heel to anyone.

Not even Cindy, who'd proved to be a good friend.

After a hearty meal of meat loaf, green beans and baked potatoes loaded with farm-fresh butter, sour cream and chives, Cindy blotted her lips and placed her napkin on the table.

"How about dessert?" Blake asked. "Maybe

some of the fresh peach cobbler or that blue-berry pie?"

"It sounds good, but I'm stuffed. Maybe I can have a bite of yours."

"Sure."

But before they could attract the attention of their waitress, the sheriff entered the diner and, when he spotted Blake, strode over to their table.

Trace McCabe, a handsome man in his late twenties, looked all-American with a military edge. He extended his hand. "It's good to see you, Blake. I've been meaning to thank you for riding in this rodeo. I know you usually compete in bigger ones than this."

"I'm glad to help."

When the sheriff looked at Cindy, she smiled. He lifted his hat, the way a gentleman was prone to do when greeting a lady. He grinned, but there seemed to be something odd in his expression. A lack of recognition, she suspected. Or maybe her makeover had just stunned him. It was hard to tell.

"You know Cindy Tucker," Blake said, as though he figured Trace needed some kind of introduction.

"Yes, I do." He flashed her a more natural smile. "That new hairdo threw me for a minute."

"Excuse me." A woman's voice sounded from a few tables away. "Sheriff, I'd like to have a word with you."

Trace turned, and so did Blake and Cindy.

It was Bitsy Dupres, a slender, forty-something blonde who wore her hair pulled into a prim and tidy bun.

When Bitsy had the sheriff's attention, she said, "We need to do something about those two old men who sit in front of the courthouse. Their very presence on that bench is a blight on our lovely park."

"It's a public bench," Trace told her. "Dutch and Buster can sit anywhere they like."

"I understand the legal predicament," she said, "but perhaps we can relocate them to a more...suitable spot."

When the woman set aside her menu, Trace glanced at Blake, revealing a hint of frustration in his eyes. Obviously, the self-appointed do-gooder had been giving him fits about one thing or another.

Blake leaned toward Cindy and quietly asked, "Who is she?"

"Bitsy Dupres. She's one of the more vocal members of the Committee for Moral Behavior."

"I can see that," Blake said. "Just where

the heck does she want to move Dutch and Buster?"

Cindy shrugged. "Probably into one of the other counties, I imagine."

Voices stilled as folks strained to hear the conversation between the sheriff and Bitsy.

But at that moment, Fred and Cassie Twain entered the restaurant with their six-year-old twins and joined Bitsy, taking their seats at her table.

Trace greeted the Twains, then used the opportunity to escape with grace and style.

"I'll catch up with you later," he told Blake. "I've got to run."

Then he ordered a cup of coffee to go and slipped out of the diner.

"Who are they?" Blake asked, nodding toward the Twains. "More members of the committee?"

"Yes and no."

"What do you mean?"

Cindy glanced at the woman with bobbed mousy hair. "That's Cassie Twain, the mayor's real estate partner. She's on the committee. And the man is her husband, Fred. He's the county assessor and works at the bank." Cindy flashed Blake a smile. "Fred's a member of the fair board."

"That ought to put a little pressure on a marriage."

"Or on the board," Cindy said. "The Twains lost money in that real estate swindle two years ago."

The waitress returned to their table, and Blake ordered a peach cobbler. Moments later, she placed a hefty serving of the homemade dessert in front of him.

"Do you want some?" he asked Cindy.

"You bet." She reached for her spoon and scooped out a goopy bite.

They sat in the corner booth, almost like a couple on a date. But Cindy knew better than to let her imagination get the better of her. Still, she couldn't help but wonder what it would be like if Blake lived in Blossom. Or what it would be like if he just came home more often than he did. He'd been determined to leave town when he turned eighteen, but maybe time had changed his mind.

Unable to keep her curiosity at bay, she asked. "Would you ever consider settling in Blossom? You know, maybe buy a house or a ranch here? For those times you're not on the circuit?"

He shook his head. "No. I like my tumbleweed lifestyle just fine. Besides, I'm not the kind of man who will ever settle down. Especially in a place that's dividing into two opposing sides, neither of which would ever fully welcome me with open arms."

She started to object, to tell him it wasn't true. But they both knew he'd never really been accepted in Blossom before. Not until he'd started winning an admirable number of rodeo belt buckles.

But at least Cindy had him in town long enough to help her snag Robby's attention.

After dinner, Blake and Cindy strolled out of the diner and down the sidewalk toward the parking lot on the backside of the courthouse, where they'd left the pickup. Blake carried the plastic bag that contained the meal they were taking home to Tuck.

In front of the Mercantile, an attractive brunette dressed in a colorful gypsy-style skirt stood before the window, staring at the mannequins on display. Cindy had never seen the woman before but found her interesting, especially because of her choice of clothes.

As they approached, the brunette turned suddenly, bumping into Blake with an audible oomph. She grabbed his arm, as though steadying herself. Their gazes locked, and they stood transfixed, yet the woman seemed to be looking right through Blake. Almost as though she was in some sort of trance.

"Are you hurt?" Blake asked.

She slowly shook her head, her thick brown curls dancing upon her shoulders. "No, but you are."

"I'm fine." He tossed her an unaffected smile. "No harm done."

"Not now," she said. "In the past. And I don't mean from being thrown off bucking broncos or the high-school brawl that caused a bloody nose, a bruised rib and a black eye."

Cindy's mouth dropped. The woman, a stranger in town, couldn't have possibly known about the fight Blake had been involved in when he was a sophomore at Sam Houston High. But she'd certainly described his injuries.

Something magical seemed to swirl around the cowboy and the brunette, something Cindy could almost touch.

The attractive woman dropped her hand. "I'm sorry. I don't usually say things like that."

"Who are you?" Cindy asked.

"Cherry Cooper. I was just checking out the town." She took a deep breath, then slowly blew it out. "Again, I'm sorry about running into you."

Then she flashed them a smile, turned and walked away, her colorful skirts swirling at her feet like the wind blowing through the trees at the height of autumn.

"That was really weird," Blake said.

"I know. She must be psychic or something."

"Ah, come on," he scoffed. "You don't believe that stuff, do you?"

"Don't you? I thought visions were a strong part of your culture."

"Maybe my father's culture, but not mine. I hardly knew the guy. Or his people."

"Well," she said. "Whether you believe it or not, there was something going on. Something unexplainable."

He nudged her with his elbow. "Come on. Let's get dinner back to Tuck before he gets tired of waiting on us and opens a can of pork and beans."

"Okay." Cindy tried to match Blake's quickening strides, while stepping carefully in the brand-new shoes that made it hard to walk without wobbling. "But that woman knew about that fight you had in high school."

"Don't get carried away."

"She even knew about your injuries. You came home battered, with two black eyes and a bloody nose. Remember? And I helped clean you up."

"You've always had a vivid imagination, Sprout. And you're too darn gullible. That's what's got me worried about some sweet-talking guy turning your head."

Cindy crossed her arms, but she kept her mouth shut. Blake could say whatever he wanted, but that woman—Cherry Cooper— had a gift. And she'd *seen* something that had happened years ago.

At a high-school football game, a couple of guys from Springdale High had taunted Blake about something. And Blake had taken them all on. If Trace McCabe and Jason Strong hadn't stepped in to help, Blake might have been hurt worse than he was.

Cindy hadn't gone to the game; she'd been too young. And Grandpa had already gone to bed by the time Blake returned home, battered and bruised. So she'd been the one to tend his wounds.

She'd always believed he'd toughed it out in front of the other guys. But at home, in the quiet of the kitchen, tears had welled in his eyes.

She'd sensed his wounded spirit then. And she'd offered him the comfort of an embrace, which he'd momentarily accepted. But he'd quickly shaken off the display of affection, like a dog climbing out of a swimming hole. And he'd taken on a tough-guy attitude that had followed him for the next couple of weeks.

No. Cherry had been right. Blake was wounded, in spite of what he said, and Cindy's heart ached for the pain he hid.

Somehow, some way, she would help him heal—if he'd let her.

Chapter Four

A couple of days later, while Blake cleaned out the stall where Cutter had spent the night, he began making a list of chores that needed to be done—things he could do to make life easier on the old cowboy who'd become his father figure.

The barn door squeaked and moaned as it swung open, and Blake made a mental note to add "oil hinges" to his list. He glanced up from his work, expecting to see Tuck, but it was Cindy who strode inside.

The *new* Cindy.

Her bright-eyed smile and yellow sundress made her look as fresh and cheery as a patch of daffodils fluttering in the breeze.

With the sunlight at her back, dust and particles of straw danced around her like fairy dust, making her transformation appear even more magical than it had yesterday. And for the life of him, he had a hard time finding the words to speak.

But he'd be darned if he'd tell her—*again*—how pretty she looked, which seemed to be the only thing that came to mind whenever he sneaked a glance at her.

"Going somewhere?" he asked.

"No. Just practicing."

He nodded, as though it made perfect sense to get all dressed up just to hang around the ranch. "I didn't see you at breakfast."

She flashed him a one-dimpled smile and pointed to the glossy curls that hung over her shoulders. "It took me a while. Charlene at the Cut N Curl gave me a few pointers, but fixing my hair wasn't as easy as she seemed to think it would be."

"Looks like you're getting the hang of it." He tossed her a half smile, but couldn't help scanning the length of her—a second time.

The effort she'd spent getting dressed was well spent, but he kept the thought to himself.

She shifted her weight to one foot, a move that reminded him of the old Cindy. Then she crossed her arms, causing her breasts to swell and stretch beyond the scooped neckline of her dress, taunting him in a way the old Cindy never had.

Damn.

"Are you busy?" she asked.

He shrugged. "Not really."

"Then can I ask you a favor?"

She wasn't carrying a jar, so she didn't need him to unscrew a tight lid.

He leaned the pitchfork against the wall and wiped his hands against the sides of his denim-clad thighs. "Sure. What do you need?"

"Will you teach me how to dance?"

Huh? Blake nearly choked on his reply. "Me?"

"Yes. *You.* I can't ask Grandpa again. It seems the jitterbug and the waltz are the only steps he knows. And what are the chances that Robby will know how to dance like they did in the forties or fifties?"

"Slim to none."

"So you're my best bet." She had a point. But what did he know about giving lessons?

"I'm not a very good dancer," he told her, although he'd never had any complaints.

"You've got to be better than I am." She blew out a sigh, which drew his attention back to the swell of her breasts.

Maybe he ought to suggest she drop her arms and keep her hands to the side. Either that or go back to wearing her tomboy garb whenever he was around.

He didn't like the way his mind drifted when she dressed like a woman who was ready, willing and able. Especially since he doubted she was prepared to handle a relationship yet, even with Robby.

"The only dance steps I learned were in P.E. when Mrs. Lassiter taught us to promenade and allemande left."

On rainy days, Mrs. Lassiter, the girls' P.E. teacher, had somehow managed to talk Coach Grider into letting her teach a coed square-dance class in the gym. Apparently, the practice had remained in effect, even after Blake had graduated.

"And that's not going to do me any good now." Cindy flipped a strand of hair over her shoulder—a new-Cindy move that was sexier than she probably realized. "So what do you say?"

"I can't teach you to dance."

"Why not?"

He opened his mouth to offer an explanation, one he hadn't completely considered, but as disappointment washed over her face, dousing the light in her eyes, he clamped his jaw shut.

Oh, what the heck. He blew out a weary sigh of resignation. "All right. I'll give it my best shot."

She beamed, then marched over to the built-in shelf on the wall near the old refrigerator and fiddled with the age-yellowed plastic knob of Tuck's clock radio. As a traffic report blasted, postponing the lesson until a song played, she moseyed back to him, hands clasped behind her back, the yellow fabric of her dress the color of a flashing caution light.

Careful, boy.

As she eased close to him, she nibbled on her bottom lip, a habit she'd always had. But it had never affected him before. Never drew him to her lips, making him realize how kissable they were.

The smell of her shampoo, something floral and fresh, blended with her orange-blossom scent and swirled in the air, stirring up all kinds of things best left alone. Like hormones. And pheromones. And inappropriate thoughts about Tuck's granddaughter.

A flood of warmth shot through Blake's veins, kicking up his pulse a notch and releasing a rush of testosterone.

What in the heck had he gotten himself into?

Cindy's nerves fluttered, as Blake's possum-in-the-flashlight gaze locked on hers.

If she didn't know any better, she'd think that he was nervous and afraid to touch her. But she *did* know better. He was just an old friend doing her a favor.

Still, she couldn't stem the thrill of dancing with a man who'd painted a swath of color through her adolescent dreams, and anticipation sent her heart topsy-turvy.

When the music started, she expected a lively beat, something that allowed him to teach her the boot-scootin' boogie or the Texas two-step.

But as Faith Hill sounded over the airwaves, singing "Breathe" with a slow beat and a sultry voice, Cindy feared Blake would nix the dance lesson.

Instead, he lifted his arms.

If her hormones were stirring before, they were surging now.

As she eased closer, he suddenly balked. "I can't touch you. I'll get you all dirty."

"That's okay. It'll wash out." She slid her arms around his neck, letting him know that she wasn't afraid of the dirt or dust or anything else that might linger long after the lesson had ended.

"This is crazy," he said. But he didn't step back. He just muttered something under his breath and wrapped her in his arms.

She wasn't sure why dancing with her seemed "crazy" to him, because as she fell into his embrace, it seemed like the most natural thing in the world.

Their steps were awkward at first, with Cindy holding on tight and trying not to step on his boots.

"Relax," he told her. "And don't think. Just let go and feel the music."

She wasn't sure about letting go, because while he held her, with Faith singing, she feared her knees would buckle. But as she leaned into him, she began to follow his lead.

As they swayed to the sensual sounds of the love song, Cindy closed her eyes and savored Blake's scent. His heartbeat lulled her. His cheek nuzzled her hair, and his hands slid over the curve of her back.

She could have sworn he was caressing her. That the words of the song had carried him to a place where he imagined holding one of the buckle bunnies who'd been pursuing him—

the "one in particular" he'd mentioned when he first arrived.

Cindy wasn't stupid. She knew better than to let romantic fantasies turn her head, especially with a man like Blake.

But for the time it took the disc jockey to play one song, she could almost believe that she belonged to him.

And that he belonged to her.

Talk about a rush.

After the last chords of the music had faded, Blake continued to hold her.

But then, as though realizing he'd been daydreaming about someone else—the *one in particular,* no doubt—he stepped back abruptly and dropped his arms. "You don't need any more lessons. You're doing fine."

But he didn't seem to be doing very well. He appeared scattered. Bothered. And he had a screwy look on his face. She couldn't quite get a handle on the expression, so she asked, "What's the matter?"

"Nothing." He ran a hand through his hair, then turned to snatch the pitchfork from the wall.

She didn't believe him, yet she didn't want to push or pry. What if he told her something she didn't want to hear, like *one in particular* might not like him dancing with another woman, even if the other woman was just Cindy.

Just Cindy.

She didn't like the way it sounded. The way it felt to compete with *one in particular*.

"Thanks for the lesson," she said.

"No problem." He slid her an easy smile, which made her wonder if she'd misread the signals.

That wouldn't surprise her. The male/female stuff always did confuse her—except in the movies, when she had the background music to give her a clue. So she decided to take him at his word. To believe that giving her a lesson hadn't been a problem at all. "I don't suppose we could try one more dance."

"Not today." He nodded toward the stall, which looked clean to her. "I've got too much to do."

"Then another time?"

"Yeah. Sure."

She tossed him a carefree smile that felt anything but, then turned and walked away.

As she approached the barn door, she sensed his eyes on her back and glanced over her shoulder to appease her curiosity.

Sure enough, their gazes locked momentarily. Then he turned away, just as quickly as their eyes had met, making her wonder if she'd imagined the entire five minutes she'd spent in the barn.

And thinking that maybe she had.

As Blake repaired the latch on the corral gate, he dropped the wrench and swore under his breath. He'd never been the least bit clumsy, but after holding Cindy in his arms, he couldn't seem to keep his mind on his work.

That simple little dance they'd shared had become too much like foreplay, whether Cindy knew it or not.

But Blake had certainly gotten the hint. And so had his libido.

Had she known what was happening—on his part, anyway?

He doubted it. She was too innocent, too inexperienced. After all, she'd asked for another dance lesson.

And like an adolescent suffering from a hormone overdose, he'd agreed.

What an idiotic response that had been. One more time in Cindy's arms and he'd be toast, especially with music-to-make-love-by whispering in his ear.

Maybe staying on the Tumbling T until the rodeo wasn't such a good idea—not if he couldn't keep things in perspective. Or his libido in check.

"Lunch is ready," Cindy called from the front porch.

He nodded to acknowledge her words, but continued to secure the last bolt by tightening the nut in place.

If he weren't so darn hungry, he would have declined lunch. But that didn't mean he would contribute to the mealtime chatter.

Ten minutes later, he sat at the kitchen table with Tuck and Cindy, trying to focus on a bowl of canned chili beans and a cheese sandwich. The food was plain but filling, and even a slice of cheese between two slices of bread hit the spot.

"By the way," Tuck said to Blake, "while you were out in the south pasture, your mother called. She'd like you to call her back."

Blake merely nodded, afraid to encourage a lunchtime conversation he didn't want to take part in—and not just because the subject of his mother had come up.

Actually, he'd expected his mom's call. She'd probably found the house she wanted to buy. Blake had offered her the down payment and promised to co-sign on the loan. He'd meant the financial assistance to appease her. But for some reason, now that she'd hit her mid-forties, she thought their relationship ought to be more than it was.

Too bad she hadn't wanted more from their relationship when he really needed a mother.

A couple of years ago, she'd even quit drinking, a serious problem she'd kept hidden from everyone in the world but him. And she'd started attending church weekly and talking about things like forgiveness and renewing broken relationships.

But heck. Their relationship was just fine, as far as he was concerned. So he'd offered to help her buy a house on Mother's Day.

Didn't that prove he'd forgiven her for all the hateful things she'd said to him when she was face-deep in the bottle?

You were always your father's child. Not mine. You're just like him.

Before he could wallow in the past any longer, Cindy's voice drew him back to the present.

"I've got a call in to the vet, Grandpa. Rebel Sky's yearling got tangled up in some old barbwire that had been buried near the stream, and I've doctored it the best I can. But I think Dr. Dobbins ought to take a look."

"Whatever you think is best," Tuck said. "You get that wire picked up and hauled off?"

"Yeah. And I've got the colt stabled in the barn for now. But I think it might be a good idea to clear the field of horses until I can make sure it's all gone."

Blake continued to eat, to keep his thoughts to himself. At times he worried that the ranch was too much for one man and his granddaughter to work alone, without an occasional hired hand to help out. But from what he'd seen, Cindy was holding her own.

She was a damn good horsewoman. Always had been. And it seemed she was determined to be all the help Tuck needed.

When she was just a kid, more times than not, she'd come straight home from school, tossing her books aside to saddle a horse and join her grandfather at work. In fact, Blake suspected she'd given up a lot during her childhood, like friends and extracurricular activities, just to make life easier on her grandpa.

The old man was lucky to have her.

Any man would be, he supposed.

When Blake finished his meal, he excused himself from the table, rinsed off his dishes and left them in the sink.

Then he reached into the front pocket of his plaid shirt, pulled out his list and waved it like a white flag. "I've got work to do."

"There's no hurry," Tuck said as Blake retreated to the service porch.

"Yes, there is." Blake took his hat off the peg by the back door. "There's a lot you need help with, and I won't be here very long."

Then he opened the back door and let himself out.

Cindy studied the door after Blake left, aware that something was bothering him.

Was he feeling guilty or weird about dancing with her?

Or had he been stewing about something before she'd even stepped foot into the barn? He hadn't been very talkative when she'd first walked in and found him cleaning stalls.

"Blake was awfully quiet," she said, prompting Grandpa for his two cents.

"He gets moody sometimes. Don't you remember?"

Yes, she did. But she'd hoped his growing fame on the rodeo circuit had knocked off the chip he'd always worn on his shoulder.

Her thoughts drifted to the wounds that the psychic had mentioned, the wounds Cherry claimed Blake still carried.

Cindy didn't know why she'd neglected to

consider how badly he must have been hurt in the past or how he might still be hurt.

What she *did* know was that Blake's grandfather had served in the army with her grandpa, while stationed at Fort Benning. And that the man—Sam—had asked Grandpa to take in his only grandchild, when Blake had been giving his single mother fits.

As a kid, she hadn't been that curious about Blake's background. And then, after he'd lived with them for a while, it hadn't seemed to matter. But now she wanted to know more about him, about where he came from. And she wanted to know who had hurt him.

It was, she realized, the only way she could help him heal.

So, while she had Grandpa alone, she decided to ask.

"Why did Blake's grandfather send him to live with us? Why didn't he take him in and give him the guidance he needed?"

Tuck ran a finger along the outside of his glass of iced tea, drawing a line in the moisture that had gathered, then looked up. "Sam had just found out he had lung cancer, so he wasn't sure he'd be around long enough to see Blake through his teen years. And he was right about that. He died a few months after Blake came to the Tumbling T."

Cindy placed her elbows upon the table and leaned forward. "What do you know about his father?"

"According to Sam, Clint Gray Feather was a gambler and a ladies' man who broke Blake's mother's heart. But I always figure there are two sides to every story."

"What do you mean?"

"I haven't talked to Blake's mother in years. But when I did, she seemed kind of cold and uninterested."

Cindy had never met the woman. And now that she thought about it, she found that odd. Of course, Susan Gray Feather had called periodically to talk to Blake, like she did today.

"Sam told me Susan was pretty hard on Blake growing up. He figured that's why the boy finally rebelled and gave her a bushel of trouble."

Cindy started to question her grandfather further, but he scooted his chair back and picked up his dirty bowl.

"Where are you going?" She figured he planned to help Blake with that list of chores. Or see about the mare that was expected to foal.

"I've got to go to the doctor," he said. "And I need to shower and clean up."

He was going to the doctor?

Again?

Cindy's heart thundered in her chest like the pounding hooves of a frightened herd. "Is something wrong?"

"Nope. It's just a little checkup. That's all. I haven't seen a doctor in years, so it's about time I did."

"But that's not true," Cindy countered. "I heard you'd been down to the clinic twice recently. And you didn't even tell me about it."

Grandpa slapped his weathered hands on his hips. "Who's been running off at the mouth?"

"Dutch and Buster."

He shook his head. "I'll have to give those old buzzards heck for getting you all stirred up about nothing."

"I'm not stirred up about *nothing*. I love you, Grandpa. And I'm concerned about your health."

"Don't worry about me." He shot her a grin that softened the craggy wrinkles on his face. "I'm as fit as a bluegrass fiddle on a Saturday night. I just went down to the clinic to make an appointment. That's all."

"Dutch and Buster said you'd been there twice."

"That's because they made me come back in for a blood test and one of those stress tests." He winked. "Got me an A plus on the treadmill. Darn thing couldn't keep up with me."

She didn't believe him. "I'm going with you to the doctor's office anyway. And I'm going to sit in the waiting room while you get your exam."

"Suit yourself."

Then he left her alone in the kitchen to worry about the two men she loved, either of whom she could lose at the drop of a worn-out cowboy hat.

An hour later, after asking Blake to wait for the vet, Cindy sat next to her grandfather in the crowded waiting room of the Lone Star Clinic. She was glad the sweet but stubborn old man had finally made an appointment for a physical, something he'd put off for the past five years.

The fact he'd showered and put on a clean shirt and pants hadn't surprised her. But the cologne was another story. He'd slapped on something different, something that actually smelled pretty good, not the usual drugstore-brand he wore to the occasional wedding or funeral.

And to add to her concern, as they'd headed for the pickup to drive to town, he started whistling a jaunty tune she didn't recognize.

Now they sat in the midst of a full waiting room that seemed to get more crowded by the minute. Were the doctors always this busy on a Friday afternoon?

When someone's name was called, a chair became vacant but didn't remain empty very long.

When Grandpa cleared his throat, something that made Cindy wonder if those unfiltered cigarettes he used to smoke had finally come back to haunt him, she lowered the *Reader's Digest* to her lap and took a concerned peek at the man who'd raised her, at the man she would stick by, through thick and thin, through sickness and health.

He sat up straight, looking at a blonde nurse who stood in the doorway that led to the exam rooms.

The woman glanced at the file in her hands, then called out, "Benjamin Tucker?"

"That's me." Grandpa quickly stood, threw back his shoulders and marched to the door.

The arthritis he sometimes complained about had flown by the wayside.

Had Dutch and Buster been right? Was Grandpa interested in a nurse who worked here?

No way. Grandpa didn't have a romantic bone in his body. And besides, *that* particular nurse was a good ten or fifteen years younger than her grandfather.

"Excuse me," a woman said. "Is that chair taken?"

Cindy glanced up to see Cherry, the attractive brunette she and Blake had run into last night. "No, it's not."

Cherry, who wore a pretty pink sundress that looked a lot like the one the mannequin in the Mercantile window had displayed, took Grandpa's seat.

"That's a pretty dress," Cindy said.

Cherry smiled. "Thank you. It caught my eye last night, which is one reason I was distracted and bumped into your friend. I went back to the dress shop this morning, after it opened, and bought it."

Cindy fiddled with the corners of the pages of the magazine in her lap, wanting to make conversation with the woman who had a psychic gift. "Did you move here recently?"

"Not yet. I'm planning to move my disabled grandmother to Blossom, and I came to check out the town." The attractive brunette nodded toward the reception desk. "And I have an appointment to speak to a doctor about her medical needs."

"It's a good clinic," Cindy said. "At least that's what I've heard."

Cindy nibbled her lip, wondering how to broach the subject of Cherry's vision.

"I'm sorry about what happened last night," Cherry said, as though reading Cindy's mind.

Had she?

Cindy found the woman intriguing. "Why are you sorry?"

"I sometimes have…visions…but I don't usually reveal them like that." She brushed a corkscrew curl away from her cheek. "But when I touched your friend, the vision was so strong that I blurted it out."

"Blake didn't think anything of it," Cindy said. "But I did. After a high-school football game, some guys on the opposing team jumped him and beat him up. And you knew exactly how he'd been hurt."

"In that brawl, yes. But the vision I had was of the wounds he carries in his heart."

"Can I do anything to help him heal?"

The woman smiled. "Not really. That's something he'll have to do on his own. And right now, he's not willing."

Cindy wasn't sure what to say, so she remained silent.

"Just love him," Cherry added.

Love him? Cindy already did. But Cherry would have to read her mind to hear an admission like that. And the fact that she may have already done so triggered another thought.

Maybe Cherry would know whether Grandpa was as healthy as he thought he was.

"This might sound weird," Cindy said. "But can you tell me whether my grandfather is all right? He's having a physical, and I'm worried about him."

Cherry grinned, her eyes sparkling. "You'll have to wait for the doctor's diagnosis."

"Don't you know?"

"I don't always get a reading on things," Cherry said, "nor can I make a vision appear."

"Well, I just had to ask. I'm worried because he used to smoke two packs a day and has never watched his diet very well. I'm afraid of what the doctor might say."

"I don't have a clue what his tests will reveal, but I can tell you this," Cherry said with a knowing expression. "Your grandfather has the heart of a young man."

"That's good to know." Cindy returned Cherry's smile. "You know, I think it's fascinating that you've been blessed with the gift of sight—or whatever it is. Do you give readings to people?"

"Yes, I do. I'm known as Lady Pandora professionally. And I travel with the carnival that's contracted with the Blossom County Fair Board."

"That's wonderful!" Cindy could barely stand the excitement. Or the desire to have Lady Pandora give her a personal reading. "Can you see my future? I'd be happy to pay you."

Cherry studied her for a moment. "You don't need to pay me. Give me your hands."

Cindy did as she was told, her fingers and palms quickly warming to Lady Pandora's touch.

Blake could scoff all he wanted, but this woman had a real gift. And unlike the phony-baloney fortune-teller who'd come to town two years ago, Lady Pandora was on the up-and-up.

As Cindy waited for a revelation of fame and fortune, Lady Pandora released her hands and smiled.

"What did you see?" Cindy asked.

"You're going to win a well-deserved prize at the county fair," the woman said.

"A prize?" Cindy asked, afraid she'd misunderstood.

"One you don't think you deserve." Cherry smiled. "And you're going to shine throughout the entire event."

Chapter Five

Cindy couldn't believe her good fortune.

Someone else might not think a blue ribbon was any big deal, but Cindy had never won anything that mattered, although she'd come close, when she was a senior in high school.

Mrs. Lassiter had encouraged Cindy to try out for the girls' volleyball team, even though she was one of the shortest girls in class. Usually, Cindy refused to get involved in after-school activities, since she had to go home and help her grandfather on the ranch. But he'd just hired a temporary hand, so Cindy had decided to give it a try.

But a week before tryouts, she'd been help-

ing Grandpa bring in a herd and was thrown
from her horse. A broken wrist ended her
dreams of shining on the team and having a
winning season, not to mention gaining her
teammates' respect.

Until today.

Maybe this was God's way of making it up
to her. Of giving her a chance at glory.

Cindy could hardly believe it. She was going
to be a winner at the fair. No ifs, ands or buts
about it. Lady Pandora had already proved herself to Cindy, and this revelation had to be
true, too.

But before Cindy could quiz the pretty psychic further, the same blonde nurse who'd
taken Grandpa back to the exam rooms called,
"Cherry Cooper."

The intriguing brunette stood. "Well, I'd
better go. It was nice talking to you."

"Same here," Cindy said. "Thanks for the
reading."

"My pleasure."

As the curly-haired psychic disappeared
behind the back office door, Cindy wondered
what she was supposed to call the woman—
Cherry or Lady Pandora?

Were they actually friends who were on a

first-name basis? Or had they shared a professional/client sort of thing?

Money hadn't changed hands, so the reading had been complimentary.

While Cindy couldn't exactly consider the psychic her friend—yet—she certainly liked the woman. *A lot.* And not just because of the positive reading. Cherry had treated Cindy with more respect than most women did.

True, the popular girls in high school treated her better after they'd all graduated. But that didn't mean she felt particularly close to any of them. If she'd had time to develop any real friendships, it would have been with Tammy Wright or Elizabeth Dupres, both of whom were kind to everyone.

She was hopeful that things would be different now that, thanks to Blake, Cindy had made some big changes in her appearance. Maybe she could be respected for more than being able to out ride or out rope most people she knew, a talent she'd tried to downplay ever since Grandpa had suggested she might do well on the rodeo circuit.

But there was no way she'd leave him. Not when he needed her on the ranch.

Of course, that didn't mean she couldn't compete in something else.

Her thoughts drifted back to the prophecy, and she couldn't help but smile.

Cindy Tucker was going to be a winner.

Of course, Cherry hadn't revealed the event, so Cindy would have to give her entry some serious thought.

She didn't have any animals to show. But then again, when a pig, goat or cow won a blue ribbon, the owner received the prize, but the animal was the real winner. So scratch that event.

Cooking and baking were out of the question. And so was woodwork. She couldn't sew a stitch. Or quilt. Or knit. So the possibilities were certainly narrowing, with nothing viable in sight.

Before she could stew on it too long, Grandpa came strolling into the waiting room wearing a big, ain't-I-somethin' grin.

"What did Dr. Tanner say?" she asked.

"He said if I was any healthier, I'd have to see a specialist for a second opinion." Then the old man chuckled at his wit.

Cindy laughed, too, convinced that her grandfather was in excellent health, in spite of nearing seventy. After all, Lady Pandora had said he had a young man's heart.

She stood, and Grandpa slipped an arm

around her as they left the clinic. Once outside, they headed for his pickup.

"Let's go out tonight," he said. "I feel like celebrating my good health."

"That's a great idea." Cindy had something else to celebrate, too—the blue ribbon she would win.

All she had to do was figure out an event in which she could handily beat out the competition.

The rodeo came to mind again, but she quickly discarded that thought. After all, Cherry had said she'd shine at the fair. And if Grandpa thought she had any desire to compete on horseback, he'd start urging her to spread her wings again, something she refused to do. Not when they were a team. A family.

Cindy was all he had on earth, other than his horse and the Tumbling T.

As she slid into the passenger side of the pickup, she still hadn't decided on an event to enter. But as soon as she got home, she'd come up with something.

And she couldn't wait to share her good news with Blake.

Blake had just finished putting Cutter through his paces and was brushing him down when he heard Tuck's pickup head toward the house. Shep, the cattle dog, had been sleeping in the shade of the barn. He barked once in welcome, then got up and trotted to the truck.

As the old cowboy and his red-haired granddaughter climbed from the Ford, they greeted Blake.

"Did the vet stop by yet?" Cindy asked.

"Yeah. He said you did a great job tending those wounds. He also gave the filly an antibiotic."

"Good." Tuck nodded toward the house. "I've got to get out of these dress clothes. I'll be back in a minute. I want to round up that brood mare and corral her closer to the house. She's going to foal soon."

"I checked her while you were gone," Blake said. "She's doing okay, but I think you're right about bringing her in."

As Tuck disappeared inside, Cindy made her way to the corral. The sun glistened off the golden highlights woven into her red hair, and the daffodil-yellow fabric of her dress fluttered like a curtain in the breeze.

Blake watched her approach, finding it hard to do anything else. He still hadn't gotten used to seeing the new Cindy. But that didn't mean he didn't like looking at her.

She tossed him a dazzling smile. "Can I talk to you about something?"

He was almost afraid to ask what. Her requests hadn't been easy ones lately. But even though he'd been intending to keep to himself for the rest of the day, he couldn't tell her no. "Sure. What's on your mind?"

"I'm going to enter something in the fair."

Blake slipped off the halter and gave Cutter a pat on the rump, letting the gelding know he was free to wander about the corral. "That seems a bit out of the ordinary for you. What makes you want to compete in the fair?"

"You remember Cherry, that lady who bumped into you last night?"

"What about her?"

"While I was waiting for Grandpa at the clinic, I saw her. And she said I was going to win something at the fair."

"Ah, come on, Cindy." Blake lifted his hat long enough to run his hand through his hair. "You really don't believe that psychic mumbo jumbo, do you?"

She stood as tall as her barely five-foot stature would allow and crossed her arms, thrusting her breasts forward. "I certainly do. She's a professional fortune-teller. And her name is

Lady Pandora. And I'd bet the ranch that she'll be famous someday."

Trying to keep his gaze on the fire in her eyes and off the swell of her breasts, he scoffed. "If I believed in fortune-tellers and thought that woman had actually seen the future, I'd suggest you compete in the Fairest of the Fair contest."

In fact, he ought to suggest she enter the beauty pageant anyway. The little red-haired girl he used to harass years ago had become a real knockout.

She looked at him as though he'd just dumped a bucket of cold, muddy water on her head. "You've got to be kidding. I can't get up on stage in a swimsuit."

"Why not?"

"Because I can't compete with women like Mary Jane Coleman."

"The heck you can't." He wasn't sure who Mary Jane Coleman was, but he figured, after the makeover, Cindy could give any of the local girls a run for their money. "You stand a good chance to win."

She grimaced, clearly not convinced.

"You're just as pretty as any of the other young women who live in Blossom County."

And that was the gospel truth. "Don't sell yourself short."

"Okay," she admitted, "I've made some changes in my appearance. I can see them when I look in the mirror. But I don't *feel* pretty. And I don't even want to compete with women who've been walking in heels and sashaying their hips since the day they turned twelve."

"All you have to do is be yourself."

She blew out a ragged sigh. "That's what I'm afraid of. That when I'm up on that stage, the lights will turn on, and I'll just be plain old geeky Cindy again."

He struggled not to reach out to her, not to touch her, to cup her cheek. And by the skin of his teeth, he managed to tuck his hands two knuckles deep into the front pockets of his jeans. "I can't give you a dose of self-confidence. That's something you'll have to build on your own."

"I know." She bit down on her bottom lip, then looked up at him with eyes that glistened with unshed tears. "Having freckles and Orphan Annie hair set me up for quite a bit of teasing and a few unpleasant nicknames in school. And I never did like to see someone teased—me or anyone else. So let's just say I got into more than my share of fistfights with the pretty, popular girls."

"And that's why you won't compete with them now?"

She shifted her weight to one foot and propped a hand on her hip. "That's about the size of it. I'm not going to subject myself to the snickers. What if I took a tumble, face-first off the stage? Or what if the back of my skirt was tucked into my panties?"

Masculine curiosity pressed him to want to see her hem lifted way up in back, but sympathy for the young woman won out. "If you walked out on that stage, you'd have the other women shaking in their stilettos, Cindy Lou."

"I'd like to think you're right. But I can't get up on a stage in the middle of the town square pretending I'm someone I'm not."

Blake eased closer, placed a finger under her chin and lifted her gaze to his. "You're more woman than you know. And when the time comes, you won't have to pretend at all."

She tried to grin, and he just about fell heart-first into her eyes. Almost, but not quite.

He dropped his hand from her face and pulled back, not trusting himself to touch her. Not when his senses were spinning and his emotions were on edge.

But that didn't mean he couldn't try and comfort her with words. "I can't imagine a man in Blossom County who wouldn't choose you as the Fairest of the Fair."

"Thanks for the vote of confidence. But I can't enter a beauty pageant yet. Maybe next year."

He nodded, knowing how much she'd hoped to win a prize of some kind. She was a darn good horse-woman, but she'd never wanted to rodeo, choosing to stick close to the ranch and see about Tuck. So she'd never put in the time and effort to compete. So the Fairest of the Fair contest was the only one in which she stood half a chance.

He wished Tuck's wife hadn't passed away. Cindy needed some maternal words right now. And maybe a few lessons in the domestic sciences.

From what Tuck had said, Sue Ellen Tucker was one of the finest cooks in all of Blossom County, if not Texas.

But then Blake remembered something else. "Hey. Isn't your grandmother's old recipe box still in the kitchen cupboard?"

"Yes. Why do you ask?"

"Because you can't cook or bake, but you can read."

She suddenly brightened. "That's right! Thanks for reminding me. What a wonderful idea."

Then she gave him a quick hug. Too quick. Because as she turned to walk a way, he inhaled deeply, trying to recapture her citrus blossom scent.

And not having any luck.

Bound and determined to make Cherry's prophecy come true, Cindy dug through the kitchen cupboards to find her grandmother's recipe box.

Blake's suggestion had led to a real lightbulb moment, and she couldn't believe she hadn't put two and two together herself.

Folks in town still talked about Sue Ellen Tucker's potato salad and something called a chicken surprise. But according to Blossom County legend, Grandma's real talent was baking pies.

Cindy, of course, could barely remember her grandmother and had never learned to cook anything that didn't have detailed instructions on the box or the can. But she had the next best thing—handwritten directions from a woman whose culinary skill was renowned.

As she searched the bottom cupboard below

the wall-mounted telephone, she shoved aside a couple of outdated phone books, an old popcorn popper and a cast-iron skillet. Far in the back, she spotted the green plastic treasure chest of recipes.

Now all she had to do was choose the one that would win her a blue ribbon at the fair.

She read the tabs until she saw Pies and Pastries, then thumbed through the cards until she found Aunt Millie's Apple Pie. Cindy didn't have the foggiest idea who Aunt Millie was, but the recipe had been in the family for years. She could tell by the stains and worn edges. It was bound to be a winner.

All she had to do was follow the handwritten instructions. How tough could that be?

Of course, Grandma's penmanship was lousy. And there were a couple of oil spots that blurred the words. But Cindy could decipher most of it.

One-and-a-half cups of flour.
A half-teaspoon of salt.
One-fourth cup of cold water.
A half-cup of shortening.

She wasn't exactly sure what shortening was, just that it was white and greasy and used for baking and fried food. And since they didn't have any on hand, she reached for the lard, which Grandpa kept in the pantry to use when he made refried beans.

Imagine that. She wouldn't even need a trip to the grocery store for the ingredients to make the crust.

If she had any qualms about that fit she'd thrown, when she refused to take home economics in high school, it would be now. But at the time, she'd found far more value in the auto shop class her counselor had tried to talk her out of taking.

Since she could cook most anything she or Tuck wanted to eat, as long as it came in a box or a can, she figured learning how to tune up the pickup would do her a heck of a lot more good. Of course, they didn't offer a blue ribbon for the fastest speed in changing engine oil.

But hey. She had directions and everything she needed to bake one of Grandma's famous pies.

She took out the big yellow mixing bowl from the cupboard. And since Grandma's measuring utensils had disappeared after Cindy took them outside and made mud pies when she was six or seven, she pulled a coffee mug from the hook on the wall. She'd have to guess where the halfway point was, like she usually did when making one of those dinners in a box. Then she opened the silverware drawer and paused.

She never could remember which spoon was which. A tablespoon must be the little one that sat on the table, beside the plate. So she grabbed the larger size.

Sift flour, measure and sift with salt.

That must be a handwritten typo. Or was that *Shift flour?*

She'd already measured it and dumped it into the bowl. She supposed she could skip that step. It didn't sound important.

Cut in shortening.

Cut in it with what? Was that another typo? She'd used a spoon to dig the lard out of the mug she'd measured it in. Should she have scraped it with a knife instead? No, she'd gotten it all out.

Work water in lightly until little balls of dough just hang together in one large ball.

The glob of dough didn't mix very well. And she couldn't quite get the flour to moisten. Maybe Grandma meant a cup and a quarter of water. That had to be it.

When she had the dough good and moist, she dumped it onto a lightly floured board.

Making pies was sure messy work. But she managed to roll out a semiround circle of dough with the rolling pin.

Ten minutes later, she had finished preparing the fruit for the filling, which had been a whole lot easier than the crust. Of course, she'd had to make a little substitution. She and Grandpa didn't have green apples, but they had red—which were sweeter. And everyone knew pies were meant to be sweet. She also deleted another little item that seemed hardly necessary. Why would Grandma add lemon juice to the fruit?

At quarter to four, she flopped a semicircular dough lid on top of the filling and scrunched the edges tight. Okay, so it looked a little funny. But this was only her first try.

Forty-five minutes later, she pulled her masterpiece from the oven, realizing it didn't look like any of the pies she'd ever seen in the display case at the Bee Hive diner or the bakery. But she'd get better in time.

After all, she had more than a week to practice. And quite frankly, at least this close to opening day, baking was Cindy's only chance of making Lady Pandora's prediction come true.

Hopefully, her pie tasted better than it looked. She'd let Blake be the one to decide.

* * *

When Blake entered the smoke-filled house, he would have been worried except that Cindy stood in the kitchen as though nothing was out of sort.

"What's burning?" he asked, as he turned on the sink in the service porch and washed his hands.

A big grin lit Cindy's face. "I made a pie."

"It smells like you forgot to take it out of the oven."

"No. I watched it carefully." Cindy pointed to a golden-brown blob that cooled on the counter. "The apple filling bubbled over and burned, but the pie came out a perfect color."

The color might be perfect, but it looked like a defective volcano.

He couldn't help but smile at her gumption and her creation, as he dried his hands and entered the kitchen. His gaze returned to Cindy, who batted a strand of hair from her face with a bandaged hand. "What happened?"

"You mean this?" She lifted her right arm, glanced at the bandage on her wrist, then sighed. "I tried to clean the syrupy goop in the oven and burned myself."

"Let me see it."

She put her hand behind her back. "It's nothing."

For some reason, he wanted to make sure. Burns could be serious. He reached for her arm and, surprisingly, she didn't argue when he pulled it to him.

He carefully peeled away the white tape, then lifted the corner of the gauze and spotted a raised, red burn. It probably hurt like heck, but he didn't think it was cause for worry. "What did you put on it?"

"I soaked it in ice water for a while. Then I put mustard on it. That's Grandpa's burn remedy, and it took a lot of the pain away."

He slowly replaced the dressing, not ready to release her hand. When he glanced up, he spotted a dab of flour on her cheek and used his thumb to brush it away. But he was unprepared for the jolt of heat that shimmied along his arm, jump-starting his pulse and nearly taking his breath away.

Their gazes locked, and the glimmer in those big green eyes reached deep inside of him. Anticipation filled the air. His. Hers. Theirs.

Damn.

He couldn't get carried away, couldn't forget who Cindy was. How innocent she was. How a guy like him could take advantage of her, especially if he was planning to hightail it out of Blossom on the closing day of the rodeo.

"Hey," he said, trying to remember the old Cindy and trying to shake off the unwelcome effect the new Cindy was having on him. "How about a slice of that pie?"

She blinked, as though trying to come back to reality herself. "Oh. Sure."

He watched as she cut into the blob and served him. Then he dug in, eager to break eye contact and ignore the blood pounding in his veins.

But he didn't expect to choke on a piecrust that tasted like a patty of Play-Doh that had been left out in the sun too long.

He coughed, afraid to open his mouth for fear he'd spit or snort.

"Are you okay?"

He nodded, trying to keep an unaffected grin on his face, then sputtered out a "yum."

"You don't like it."

"It...just...went...down the..." He coughed, then reached for a glass, filled it to the brim with water and tried to force down a big swallow. "It...went down...the wrong...tube."

"You're just trying to be nice." Her smile turned upside down.

Her disappointment was nearly too much for him to bear. But what was a guy to do? Lie? Encourage her to poison the judges at the fair?

"It's okay." He forced a grin. "It's just a little saltier than I like." And harder to chomp on.

"Are you going to finish eating it?"

Think quick.

"I don't want to ruin my appetite. Tuck wants to go out to dinner. He suggested The Alibi."

She brightened. "He mentioned going out, but not where. They have dancing at The Alibi."

If Blake had a lick of sense, he'd decline dinner, especially knowing the roadside honky-tonk had a dance floor that was packed on Friday nights. But he couldn't stomach another bite of Cindy's pie. And he didn't want to hurt her feelings.

Maybe if she got caught up in the excitement of going out, she'd forget about the pie, and he could get rid of it before she tasted it. Of course, he'd stepped right into another dance lesson. But at this point, if he wanted to see her smile again, it didn't matter. "Yeah. That's right. They'll have a band playing."

"Then maybe I ought to go get dressed." She tossed him a pretty smile that didn't appear to be too wounded. "It takes me a little longer to get ready these days."

"Tuck will be coming in any minute. He

was right behind me. And knowing him, he'll be eager to go."

"I'll try to hurry."

Blake stood by the sink, watching as she left the room and wondering if he'd jumped from the skillet to the flame.

He hadn't wanted to risk dancing with her again.

But maybe, if he taught her the Texas two-step, he'd fulfill his promise to help her attract Robby's attention. And then he could leave her in Blossom and be on his way.

Even though something told him that she wasn't ready to be turned loose on the male population.

And for some dumb reason, he wasn't ready for it, either.

Chapter Six

After Cindy left the kitchen to get dressed, Blake opened the window and turned on a fan, hoping to rid the house of the burnt-apple stench.

The hinges squeaked as Tuck entered the back door, with Shep on his heels. The retired rodeo cowboy hung his hat, paused by the sink in the service porch, then peered through the doorway to the kitchen and grimaced. "What in tarnation is going on? It smells like the house caught fire."

"No need to call nine-one-one. Cindy made a pie and the filling spilled over into the oven. I'm just trying to air the place out a little."

Tuck blew out a slow whistle. "Where is she?"

"Getting dressed for dinner." Blake slid the old man a slow grin. "But go easy on her, will you? She's proud of what she made, even if it looks and tastes like heck."

"Why on earth did she go and bake a pie?" Tuck snatched a couple of paper towels from the roll and dried his hands. "I told her I wanted to go out tonight."

"She wanted to practice so she can enter the baking competition at the fair."

Tuck's attention lit on the golden-brown blob that cooled on the countertop, and he arched a bushy gray brow. "Is that it?"

Blake nodded.

"It doesn't look edible."

In spite of not wanting to make fun of Cindy's handiwork, a smile tugged at Blake's lips. "My taste buds are still rebelling. And I'm not sure if my stomach will ever forgive me."

Tuck ran a craggy, callused hand through his hair. "What would possess her to do something like that? She doesn't know how to bake anything from scratch."

"She's dead set on winning a blue ribbon at the fair. And she figured, with one of your wife's recipes, she'd be a shoo-in."

Tuck blew out a heavy sigh. "Sue Ellen could

throw an old boot into a bucket of rainwater and make it taste like a million bucks. She had a gift. And any time her friends tried out one of her recipes, it never tasted quite the same."

Blake cleared his throat and looked around, making sure Cindy was gone. "Just so neither one of us has to come up with an excuse not to have any more pie tonight, we'll be sure to order two or three desserts with our dinner."

"Good idea." Tuck eased closer to the pie, bent forward and furrowed his brow. "Looks more like a cow-pie to me. Maybe, if we accidentally knock the plate on the floor, Shep will do us a favor and eat it."

Blake looked at the dog. "I don't think he'll take more than a sniff."

"Well, let's get moving. I'd like to be at The Alibi before six."

"Why's that?"

"No reason."

Blake had a feeling Tuck was up to something, but he was hungry. And as bad as that slice of pie had tasted, it hadn't put a damper on his appetite. He was as eager to get on the road as Tuck. There were just so many beans and franks a guy could stomach, and Blake was looking forward to some decent food.

But still, The Alibi seemed an odd choice

for a meal, although the roadside diner was a great place to play a game of pool or throw some darts. And the perfect place to drink and get rowdy.

"I'm surprised you don't want to go to the Bee Hive," Blake said. "They have hearty, home-style meals and a great dessert menu."

"Nope. I have a hankering for a taste of those buffalo wings they serve at The Alibi. And I just might like to kick up my heels and dance tonight. They've got a new band that's supposed to be pretty good."

Tuck was in the mood to dance?

That Blake had to see—even if it meant he had to get out on that dance floor himself and fulfill his promise to Cindy.

At a quarter to six, Blake and Tuck sat in the living room, showered and ready to go.

"What's keeping her?" Tuck asked. "She never used to take this much time to get ready."

"She's decided to be a lady. And you know how long it takes women to get dressed."

"Too long when a man is hungry or in a hurry." Tuck chuffed. "I'm not sure I like the changes in her. Fancy clothes, trying her hand at cooking and baking. Primping and taking up too much time in the bathroom."

"I don't think you really mind the changes," Blake countered. "You've just never been very patient when it comes to waiting."

"That's for darn sure." Tuck glanced at his watch, then strode down the hall and knocked on Cindy's door. "The truck's leaving in two minutes. If you're not in it, we're going without you."

Blake was hungry, too. But he knew better than to leave Cindy at home. She could get as feisty as a little bantam rooster when provoked. And he wasn't up for any kind of tangle with her. Not when he didn't know whether to expect the old Cindy or the new Cindy to come out fighting mad.

The old Cindy he could handle. But the new one? Just looking at her made him uneasy. Apprehensive. Unbalanced.

Before Tuck could reach the front door, Cindy came out of her room and walked down the hall.

She wore that simple black dress Blake had bought her at the Mercantile, the one with the hem above the knees and a lot of her back exposed.

He hadn't wanted to buy that one—not because he didn't like it but because it was too sexy. Just looking at Cindy in that outfit was arousing. Too arousing for a family friend like Blake.

But the saleslady had oohed and aahed over it, and Cindy had pulled out her wallet to buy it herself. So he'd given in.

But for Pete's sake, he couldn't take her to the honky-tonk dressed like that. She'd have every man alive—married, single or on their way to the grave—stepping on their tongues all night.

"Wooo-eeee." Tuck chuckled. "You sure do look nice, little girl."

"I hope it was worth the wait." Cindy glanced at Blake as though hoping he'd second Tuck's opinion.

But Blake merely stared at her, hoping he didn't trip over his own tongue. But he couldn't let her leave the house like that. Not to go to The Alibi.

"What's the matter?" she asked.

"Are you going to wear *that?* Tonight?"

She glanced down at the black stretchy fabric. "What's wrong with it?"

"It's a bit dressy for The Alibi, don't you think?"

"I've never been there. I wouldn't know."

"It's a honky-tonk. Your jeans and a flannel shirt would be better." And far less likely to draw the kind of attention she wasn't ready to handle.

She furrowed her brow. "I wanted to look nice. Am I overdressed?"

"You look fine," Tuck said. "Let's go."

It wasn't her grandfather's opinion Cindy wanted. She studied Blake, noting the tension in his jaw, the intensity in his whiskey-colored gaze.

She suspected it was more than her clothing bothering him. "What's on your mind?"

"Nothing." Blake grabbed his hat and headed for the door.

After he'd walked outside, Grandpa took her aside. "You look good, Cindy Lou. *Too good.* That's all that's bothering him."

She looked *too* good? And Blake was bothered by it?

Call it crazy, inappropriate and out of line, but Cindy wanted to see just how *bothered* Blake would get this evening.

She smiled as she followed Grandpa outside. And this time, as she walked down the steps in her black heels, her legs didn't wobble at all. She was getting the hang of being a lady. And beginning to like it—a lot.

Blake was already in the cab of his truck

and had the engine running when she and her grandfather approached.

Grandpa opened the passenger door for her. "Just slide on in, Cindy Lou."

As she scooted across the seat, she tugged at the hem of her skirt to keep it in place but wasn't having much luck. She glanced at Blake, to see if he was paying any attention to her.

A scowl said he was, and she couldn't help but grin. She was having an effect on him. A sexual one, she suspected.

Maybe it wasn't as strong an effect as one of his buckle bunnies—*one in particular*—might have on him, but things were certainly looking up.

As soon as Grandpa shut the passenger door, Blake gunned the engine and headed out, tires crunching along the graveled driveway and kicking up dust.

Cindy liked sitting close to Blake, her thigh next to his, shoulders nearly touching. The scent of his cologne, something musky and light, stirred her senses, not to mention triggered her imagination.

If Grandpa hadn't been in the pickup, she might pretend they were going on a real date. And not out for burgers and fries and a Saturday matinee. But to a honky-tonk that was chock-full of adult entertainment and possibilities.

There were some life-altering changes coming down the pike. And this evening just might kick them off.

They rode in silence for about fifteen minutes, until they reached the entrance of the army-green ramshackle building that Cindy had seen on many occasions but had never entered. A flickering blue neon light dangled in the front window, announcing The Alibi was open.

Cars and trucks had already begun to fill the dusty lot, and Blake pulled up next to a red pickup with gun racks attached near the rear window.

"This place will be really hopping by nine," Tuck said.

The wooden structure didn't look like much. And it could certainly use a renovation—on the outside anyway. But Cindy had always been curious about what appealed to some and concerned others.

"The Committee for Moral Behavior has been trying to shut down the place for nearly a year," she said.

"But they aren't having much luck." Grandpa chuckled. "Things get a little out of hand sometimes. But people need a place to unwind and have a little fun."

Blake parked, and Grandpa quickly climbed out and shut Cindy inside, without giving her an option of which door to choose—not that she wanted one.

Blake held the door for her, his eyes glued on her every move as she struggled—but not very hard—to get out of the cab without showing him too much skin.

"You should have worn jeans," he told her.

She froze in midstep, half in and half out of the truck, and caught his eye. "I thought you said my legs look nice."

"They do." He scanned her thighs, her knees, her shapely calves and ankles. Then, as though realizing he was ogling her, he looked at the evening sky and muttered, "Let's just drop it, okay?"

She smiled inwardly, although her lips quivered a bit. "Can you help me down? I'm still getting used to these darn shoes."

He grumbled under his breath, but reached for her. His thumbs skimmed her tummy, which stretched the fabric of her dress, and his fingers wrapped around her waist, sending a shiver of heat coursing through her blood.

As he swung her to the ground, she sucked

in a breath. Her knees buckled a bit, and she grabbed his arm to steady herself. Their eyes locked momentarily, and awareness surged between them, silent but alive, like the air before a Texas twister roared to life.

Her heart flip-flopped, and his scowl disappeared. For one brief moment, she thought he was going to kiss her.

But he didn't.

He cleared his throat. "You okay?"

She nodded, her self-confidence soaring. Then she flashed him a smile. But instead of sending her one of his own in return, the scowl crept back on his face, and he muttered something under his breath.

He turned and headed for the entrance, leaving her to catch up. The soles of her new heels slipped against the gravel, making it difficult to walk.

She reached for his arm, grabbing his shirtsleeve instead, and pulled him to a halt. "You've got a burr under your saddle. And I'd just as soon you spit out what's bothering you here and now."

Blake didn't say anything for a moment. They just stood there eyeing each other like two kids in the schoolyard, ready to go head-to-head. Then his expression softened, and he fingered one of her curls, gave it a gentle tug and exhaled a weary sigh. "I'm sorry, Cindy. Your legs do look nice. *Too nice,* especially at a place like this."

She lifted a brow but didn't question him. She was afraid to. Was he being protective of her? Or was it something more? Something she had no business pinning her hopes on?

"Not that The Alibi is that wild or seedy," he added. "But a lot of guys who come here are looking for a good time. And you're practically advertising fun and frolic."

Was it ticking him off to think other men might find her attractive? That she appeared to be playful and ready for a good time?

She had half a notion to blow a raspberry at him, but chose a more grown-up and ladylike response. "I *am* going to have fun and frolic this evening. With or without you."

Then she headed into The Alibi, intending to enjoy her first night on the town, even if it was at a run-down honky-tonk and she had to fight Blake Gray Feather every step of the way.

Blake followed Cindy into The Alibi, just like Shep tagged along behind Tuck on the ranch.

What in the hell had just happened out there?

He wasn't sure, but if it had been a sporting event, the score was Cindy 5; Blake zip.

Once inside, her pretty head turned this way and that, taking in the seedy honky-tonk. And in spite of himself, Blake did the same.

He hadn't been in The Alibi in years. Not since he and Trace had come in here on a Saturday night and sweet-talked a waitress into serving two underage high school students a couple of beers.

Looking back, it was a wonder they hadn't gotten themselves or The Alibi in some serious trouble.

Now, as the sheriff of Blossom, Trace wouldn't tolerate underage drinking, nor would he go easy on an establishment that served minors. And he'd have Blake's full support.

That just went to show how some things had changed around here.

Even if some things, like The Alibi, hadn't.

Blake scanned the walls, noting the stuffed heads that were still mounted like artwork—deer, elk and moose. And they still kept a display of different types of barbwire, along with a photo gallery of local celebrities who'd once patronized the bar.

The back room held a couple of pool tables and dartboards, not to mention a few second-rate hustlers. And near the entrance a section of the ceiling was still missing, revealing insulation made of old egg crates held in place by chicken wire. Grady, the owner, was either too cheap to replace it or thought it was part of the honky-tonk's charm.

Cindy studied the interior with the wide-eyed expression of an innocent, a contrast to the way she strode across the scarred hardwood floor with the sexy sway of a woman who knew exactly who she was and what she wanted.

Several sets of male eyes followed her, but she didn't seem to notice.

Blake noticed the unattached men, though. And he slid each of them a don't-get-any-ideas glare, which didn't seem to go over very well.

Maybe it would be best if everyone at The Alibi thought Blake and Cindy were on a date. Of course, that would be tricky, since Blake only wanted the men on the prowl to get that idea—not Cindy.

Fortunately, Tuck chose a darkened corner booth, which got Cindy out of the limelight as soon as she joined him.

Blake sat on the cracked red vinyl seat, slid next to her and tossed her a let's-pretend-we-didn't-have-words-outside grin.

She seemed to soften a bit. At least, he hoped that was the case.

Tuck passed out the one-sided menus that were stacked on the table but didn't even look at his. Instead, he kept his eyes peeled toward the front door, as if he were expecting someone.

But he didn't have to wait very long for that someone to arrive.

"Excuse me." The retired cowboy scooted around the table and stood. "I see a friend."

"Who?" Cindy scanned the room, as though searching for someone she would recognize.

"Just a gal who's new in town." Tuck adjusted the gold buckle of his hand-tooled leather belt. "Her name is Loraine. And she has a friend visiting her. When she asked where they might go for some fun and dancing, I suggested they come here."

So the "hankering" Tuck said he'd had was for more than buffalo wings.

Blake watched the dapper old cowboy saunter toward the attractive middle-aged ladies, then escort them to a table across the room.

"Well, I'll be darned," Cindy said as she craned her neck and watched her grandpa join the women. "The blonde in the turquoise blouse is the nurse from the clinic."

"I think it's great that your grandfather is getting off the ranch and enjoying life."

Cindy returned her attention to Blake, studying him with those springtime eyes that proclaimed her innocence. "And what about you? Do you get a chance to kick up your heels and have some fun?"

"Every now and again."

"With *one in particular?*"

He furrowed his brow, completely at a loss. "With what?"

"Not with *what*. With *whom*," she corrected. "When you first came to the ranch, you said there was one woman in particular who was chasing after you. You didn't give me a name."

He wasn't so sure he wanted to discuss Jessica with Cindy, although he didn't know why. In the past, he'd been able to talk to her about most anything.

That, he supposed, was another of the things that had changed over the years.

Before he could respond, a tall waitress with bleached blond hair and dark roots stopped at the table to get their order. "What'll y'all have?"

He slid her an appreciative smile—not because he wanted a drink, but because she'd saved him from responding to a question about an old lover who'd only recently become an ex.

"I'll have a beer and an order of the spicy buffalo wings to begin with." He looked at Cindy. "How about you?"

She scrunched her nose in a cute, impish way. "I tried a beer once and didn't like it. What else do you suggest I try?"

"Soda pop," he replied, before the waitress could offer an alcoholic suggestion.

"Not in *here*," Cindy said, those lively green eyes glimmering with spunk. "I'm in a honky-tonk and want to have a *real* drink."

"How about a strawberry daiquiri?" the waitress said. "It's kind of like a fruit slush with a kick."

"Great." Cindy leaned back and grinned.

Blake couldn't help but notice the way the black material stretched across her full breasts, taunting him to forget himself and go ahead and contribute to her delinquency, even if she was no longer a minor.

The waitress returned with their drinks, and Cindy took a sip of hers.

"What do you think?" he asked.

"It's okay. But to tell you the truth, I think I'd like it better without the alcohol."

Good. At least he didn't have to worry about her kicking up her heels *and* losing her head.

Thirty minutes later, it appeared that Tuck

had permanently parked his butt at the ladies' table. He had a drink in front of him, as well as a plate piled high with a variety of appetizers.

"I think we're on our own this evening," Blake said, as he motioned for the waitress. "Let's eat."

Cindy ordered a cheeseburger and fries, while Blake chose the barbecued pork ribs, a baked potato with the works and a salad.

Instead of talking while they waited for their food, they watched the band set up. And before long, sounds of country-western music filled the room and a few couples stepped out on the dance floor.

"You promised me another dance lesson," Cindy reminded him.

Blake wasn't looking forward to dancing with her again, but he *had* promised. And a lesson in public was far better than one in private. Besides, this particular song wouldn't require him to hold her close, breathe in her scent or deal with inappropriate feelings. "All right. Let's give it a try."

By the time the band had played two sets, Cindy could manage a half-decent Texas two-step and had a handle on the boot-scootin' boogie. Even Tuck tore up the dance floor with the blond nurse, as well as her dark-haired friend.

It didn't take a mind reader to see that he was having the time of his life.

And as much as Blake hated to admit it, he'd had more than his share of laughs, too.

Between sets, he and Cindy ate dinner, which might be one reason their food had been lukewarm. The ribs were a little overcooked and greasy, but Blake didn't mind. The meal might have been a whole lot better at the Bee Hive, but the diner wouldn't have been nearly as much fun.

As the band members began to climb back on stage, Cindy excused herself to go to the rest room. And as she slid from the booth and strode across the room, practically every male in the place turned and watched, including the bartender and a tall, lanky cowboy who leaned against the bar.

While they'd been dancing, Blake hadn't paid much attention to the men who'd been ogling her earlier, but he should have. The horny gawkers seemed to be getting bolder, their interest more blatant, especially now that Cindy had left his side.

They'd probably noticed that he hadn't claimed her for a slow dance and wondered if she was free for the taking.

As the band struck up a love song, Cindy started back across the floor.

The tall cowboy near the bar took a swig of his beer, then made his way toward her. Apparently, the ol' boy wanted to find out if she was attached or not.

But Blake wasn't about to let another guy hold Cindy in his arms.

He reached her just as the cowboy did. And he flashed the guy a smile that didn't reach his eyes. "The lady is mine this evening."

"Lucky man," the cowboy said as he spun around and returned to the bar.

"Yours for the night?" Her eyes sparkled with mirth. Or maybe something else. Heck if he knew what was going on in that pretty head of hers.

"Yeah. For tonight. You're not ready for dime-store cowboys looking to hook up before closing time." He lifted his arms, hoping to end the discussion and get back on a more even keel. And, thank goodness, she stepped into his embrace and followed his lead as they moved to the slow and steady beat.

He stood nearly a foot above her, yet their bodies fit together in a pleasurable way. Soft and hard. Gentle and strong.

She'd used a different shampoo this evening.

One that had a peachy scent. He'd always had a fondness for peaches.

His fingers caressed the fabric of the back of her dress, his thumbs skimming where skin met clothes. A sense of yearning settled over him, a need to possess her, not just for this evening but every night to come.

It had to be the music. The seductive beat. The fact he had his eyes closed and couldn't see who it was that he held in his arms.

She nestled her head against his chest, near his heart. Could she hear the steady beat, pounding out an arousal he hadn't expected?

As the last chords of the song ended, he continued to hold her. And when he finally forced himself to let go, their eyes met and something slammed into his chest.

Something powerful and impossible to ignore.

Something that told him he'd better give her a long, promising kiss or hightail it out of Blossom County for good.

He swallowed—hard. Afraid to move.

And afraid not to.

Chapter Seven

Blake seemed to be rooted to the dance floor, connected to Cindy by the beat of their hearts.

His hand slowly lifted, as though it had a mind of its own, and cupped her jaw. His thumb skimmed across the softness of her cheek.

He wasn't sure what he was going to say, what he was going to do. And for one brief moment, when her lips parted, he nearly lost every lick of sense he'd ever had.

That is, until a drunken cowboy staggered onto the dance floor, bumped into him and jarred him back to reality.

He dropped his hand, tucked his thumb into

the front pocket of his jeans and cleared his throat, hoping it would clear his mind.

What had gotten into him? How could he even consider a romantic fling with Cindy?

She didn't need a cowboy who chased rodeos and traveled from town to town. She needed a family man who would settle down on her grandfather's ranch in Blossom County and give her a couple of kids.

And that man *wasn't* Blake Gray Feather.

"Thanks for the dance." His voice came out hoarse and rusty, as though he'd taken a week-long nap. "I…uh…need to get a little fresh air. Why don't you ask Tuck to introduce you to his friend."

She nodded without commenting, as though she might be just as dazed by the arousing dance as he was. But he wouldn't touch that possibility with insulated gloves.

He turned and walked away, bumping into another cowboy as he made his way to the front door.

Whew. He needed more than a breather. He needed to escape.

Blake wasn't sure how long he stood outside watching an occasional car drive by or a couple of patrons get into their vehicles and leave. Not long enough, he decided, as he walked around to the side of the building, without any idea where he was going. His boots crunched on the gravel as he tried to walk off whatever had clouded his mind. Maybe he ought to go inside and tell Tuck he was ready to leave.

But how could he do that when the older man was having a rip-roaring time?

Footsteps sounded behind him, and he turned to find Cindy.

"What's up?" she asked.

"Nothing."

She tucked a strand of hair behind her ear, revealing a pair of earrings he hadn't noticed before. A pair that didn't look new or stylish. An heirloom that had belonged to her mother maybe? Or to her grandmother?

It must be nice to have something that had been in the family for years. Something that had belonged to a parent or grandparent.

He didn't have squat to remember his dad by. And as weird as it was to admit, it bothered him that he didn't. Especially since he vaguely remembered his old man. Remembered riding on his shoulders. Sharing an ice-cream sundae.

"You're not feeling guilty about dancing with me, are you?"

He was feeling a lot of things after dancing with her, but he wasn't sure guilt was one of them. Of course, if he'd kissed her on the dance floor, like he'd been tempted to do, he'd be feeling a ration of guilt for messing with Tuck's granddaughter.

But unwilling to share his thoughts, he merely shrugged.

"Is it because of *one in particular?*"

No. Not at all. But if telling her that it *was* because of Jessica made backpedaling any easier for either of them to handle, he decided to imply that it was. "Maybe."

Cindy's heart dropped to her gut. But then, what business did she have even dreaming that Blake might be attracted to her? She'd known better from the start.

So she decided to make it easy on him, even if she had to stretch the truth. "I know just how you feel."

He cast her a skeptical look. "You do?"

She nodded. "Because of my interest in Robby. But you and I don't have anything to feel guilty about. We've been friends for a long time. So we danced and had an enjoyable evening. That's all."

The lie—at least on her part—slid easily off her tongue, but reality remained in her mind, in her heart. But it was better this way. She wasn't going to throw herself at a man who wasn't interested in her. Nor would she give Blake any idea how much she really cared about him. She wasn't about to risk losing his friendship for anything.

"Maybe you're right." He managed a smile. "So what did you think about your grandfather's friend?"

"She's nice. Her name is Loraine. But I can't imagine her and Grandpa being a match."

"Why not?"

She shrugged. "The age difference, I guess. And the fact that Grandpa hasn't had a date in more than fifteen years."

"The heck he hasn't."

Cindy's jaw dropped. "What do you mean?"

"He's had several dates that I know of. Apparently, you weren't aware of them."

She didn't know what to say. "Why didn't he tell me?"

"Men don't always reveal what they're really thinking."

Hmm. Women didn't, either, but she knew better than to admit it. Especially if she intended to maintain a friendship with Blake—a friendship she would screw up if she wasn't careful.

"Do you think your grandfather is ready to go yet?" Blake asked.

"Probably. His friends were saying they had to turn in because they had to get up early in the morning."

"Good. Then let's go home."

As they walked back to the front of the honky-tonk, Cindy looked at the sparkling, star-speckled sky. She supposed she should be happy that things were back to normal. At least it felt that way.

Earlier this evening, when she was climbing out of the pickup, she'd gotten the feeling that Blake had wanted to kiss her. Of course, she hadn't given her instinct much credit, since she still wasn't familiar with the nuances of male/female relationships.

But out on that dance floor, she'd sensed it again. Only stronger. And this time, she was going with her gut.

Blake had almost kissed her. She might still be struggling with the other sexual stuff, but she hadn't misread *that*.

In her dreams, he'd gazed longingly into her eyes a hundred times. And in reality, he'd done the same thing. But then he'd balked.

She regretted not making the first move on the dance floor. Not putting her arms around his neck and pulling his lips to hers. Because now she'd never know if his real kiss was as good as it had been in her dreams.

But making a brazen move like that would have changed their relationship for good. And she wouldn't have been able to minimize a kiss the same way she'd made light of the sensual dance they'd shared just minutes ago.

Truth and reality struck hard. Blake wouldn't want someone like her. Not when he had women like *one in particular*—or rather, Jessica—chasing after him.

No, sir. When it came to love and romance, Robby Bradshaw was a far more realistic choice for Cindy.

But the biggest piece of her heart would always belong to Blake.

Whether he wanted it or not.

It was nearing midnight when they returned to the ranch. And the smile on Grandpa's face hadn't flickered once. As he stepped onto the front porch, he paused and glanced at the new moon. "It's a pretty night."

"It sure is." Cindy looked at the bright splatter of stars in the sky. "I think I'll sit outside for a while. All that dancing has me too wound up to sleep."

"I'm going to turn in," Grandpa said. "I'll see you in the morning."

As Blake started to follow Tuck into the house, Cindy reached for his arm and stopped him. "Why don't you join me?"

He looked stumped, as though he wasn't sure if he should sit or bolt.

Stopping him from going inside may have been a mistake, but she hadn't been ready for the evening to end. Not when she knew that thoughts of Blake and the kiss they'd almost shared would keep her awake.

"I'd like to talk to you," she said, hoping something would come to mind.

He shrugged. "All right."

She took a seat on the porch swing, and he sat beside her.

"I had fun tonight," she said.

"So did your grandfather. I'd never seen him kick up his heels like that."

"Do you think he likes Loraine?" She bumped against Blake's shoulder. "You know. Romantically speaking?"

"It looked that way to me." He leaned back in the swing, the chain and wood creaking under his weight. "But not many women know how to love a cowboy."

Cindy wasn't sure what he meant by that.

But she suspected she was the exception. If given the chance, she would know exactly how to love a cowboy like Blake.

She wasn't sure when the crush she had on him had turned into the real McCoy. But it had, in spite of knowing that she'd set herself up for a major disappointment.

But isn't that why they said people *fell* in love? They didn't go looking for it. They just sort of tripped into it, ready or not. Like it or not.

Did Blake feel the same way about the woman who chased after him? Is that what he'd come to realize out on the dance floor with Cindy?

A part of her wanted to skirt the issue, but curiosity wouldn't let her keep quiet. "So tell me about Jessica."

"There's not much to tell."

Cindy doubted that. "Who is she?"

"She's a barrel racer. Nice girl. Pretty. But she wants more from me than I'm willing to give."

Cindy turned in her seat, causing the swing to sway and her knee to brush his. "Like what?"

"She wants to settle down and get married. And I'm not the marrying kind."

"Why not?"

He seemed to ponder the question, and she wasn't sure if that was because he didn't have a clear answer or whether he didn't know how to put it into words that she could understand. "A guy has to fit in, to compromise, to blend. And I've never been able to do that."

She wasn't sure what he meant. But he'd made similar comments before. Comments she hadn't put much thought into.

A bevy of goose bumps shivered up and down her arms, as though she'd hit upon something. A revelation.

A reminder of a vision.

"Do you think that has something to do with those wounds Cherry talked about?"

"What wounds? You're giving that woman more credit than you should. I'm just different. An outsider. That's all."

"I don't see you as being any different than anyone else."

"Maybe *you* don't. But I grew up being different. More like my dad's side of the family than my mom's. But even they didn't…" He stopped, as though having a revelation of his own, and looked at the Texas sky as if he was searching for something he'd never find anyway.

"You belong here," she said. "With us."

Did he?

God knows Cindy and Tuck had been good to him, but he'd still kept an emotional distance. He couldn't explain the need to do that. Just that it was there, as deep and strong as the instinct to survive.

"No, I don't fit in here, either," he said. "Not really. But I appreciate all you and Tuck have done for me. More than you'll ever know."

Blake had gained a deep respect for the older cowboy who could cuss a blue streak when someone screwed up but was able to praise a guy, too. And as pesky as Cindy had been at times, he couldn't help but care about her. A lot. In fact, he'd opened up more to her than he ever had with anyone.

She bumped her shoulder against his upper arm. "Why do I get the feeling you don't *want* to belong?"

Because, in a way, he'd quit trying to fit in. It had started when he was a child, when he'd learned he was a half-breed who felt like a misfit in either culture.

But the rodeo was a culture of its own.

"If it makes you feel better," he said, "I found my place on the circuit."

"But you have friends in Blossom. Jason Strong and Trace McCabe think of you as one of them. I've seen that raised-index-finger salute you give each other."

"You're right. Those guys are the best."

And they'd been good friends ever since the night of the fight. The night Blake had realized there was a part of him that would never belong.

"Sometimes people learn who their real friends are when the chips are down."

She had that right. When Blake had moved here as a freshman, they'd only been acquaintances at best. Trace had been two years older than Blake. The quar-terback and captain of the team. And Jason, who'd already graduated, was the assistant coach.

"You never did tell me what actually caused that fight."

He'd told her that it was one of those your-team-plays-like-a-bunch-of-girls sort of things. But those kinds of comments he could have shunned. Ignored. Or he could have fought them with a middle-finger gesture as he climbed onto the school bus to head back to town. But there'd been more to it than that.

"During the game, one of the defensive backs had been bad-mouthing me after every play. I was getting pretty sick of it. But as I was heading to the bus, he made an ethnic slur, calling me a savage. Among other things." He leaned back in the seat, causing the swing to sway. "And a lot of pent-up anger kicked into play."

"So that's when Jason and Trace stepped in?"

Blake chuffed. "No. I was actually getting the best of the guy. But a couple of his teammates stepped in to help. And when I was clearly outnumbered and facing a beating, Trace jumped in to help. The fight escalated until Jason used his authority as an assistant coach to take control of the situation. Trace and I went home pretty banged up. But not as bad as the other guys."

"See? You fit in with Jason and Trace."

"Yeah," he admitted. "That's true. But there will always be someone ready to remind me that I'm different."

Cindy supposed she could understand how he felt. She'd always been different, too. "You're not the only one who struggled to be accepted."

"I guess you're right. You never really had too many girlfriends, did you?"

"Elizabeth Dupres, Bitsy's daughter, was always nice to me. And I always considered her a friend. But we never had any classes together. And after school, I had a lot of chores to do."

She reached for the chain that held the swing to the roof of the porch and fingered the cool, hard links. "But some of the pretty, popular girls used to snicker at things I'd say or do and make fun of the clothes I wore."

"Those girls could never hold a candle to you." His knee brushed hers again, sending a jolt of heat through her blood. And as his eyes sought hers, he reached for a strand of her hair, caressed the curly lock. Then he let it slip from his fingers. "Not when it comes to loyalty and having a good heart."

"Thanks. But when I was in school, only one guy took time to look on the inside and see the real me. Or at least, that's what I'd hoped when he asked me out."

"You mean Robby?"

She shook her head. "No, he was too shy back then. But Kevin Roarke took me to the senior prom—my one and only date. But that was a disaster."

"Why?"

She shrugged, wondering how much to divulge. "Let's just say we came home with bruised toes and egos."

If she had learned anything that evening, it was that she wasn't the kind of girl teenage boys found attractive, not to mention that dating was hard work, especially when feminine wiles and flirtation didn't come naturally.

But maybe all that had begun to change. She'd noticed the male attention she'd gotten at The Alibi tonight. Of course, her focus had been on Blake.

"So you never heard from Kevin again?" he asked.

"Not other than passing him in the hall on the way to class."

"I wouldn't consider it a loss, not if he was anything like his older brother."

"He...uh...." How much should she tell him? It was pretty embarrassing. But then, if she didn't want to make the same mistake again...

"What did he do?"

For the life of her, she had a hard time admitting that she'd made the first move and kissed Kevin. And that any book she'd read or movie she'd watched in the past hadn't done her a bit of good.

Blake tensed in his seat, making the swing sway. "What the hell did that guy do?"

"Well...he didn't exactly do anything. I mean he kissed me. But it's what he said after that."

He turned, his thigh bumping into hers again, warming her again. The light from the living-room window wasn't bright enough to make out his expression, but she could feel his concern. His interest.

"Kevin said I kissed like a fish."

Blake scoffed. "Roarke ought to know, since his older brother was a known brownnoser in school. The two of them have probably kissed a lot of *bass*."

Cindy socked him in the arm. "Don't make jokes. I don't know how to kiss a guy. And I tried to do it like they did in *Top Gun*. Remember that kissing scene?"

"That sexy, openmouthed kiss? Yeah, I remember. But why would you kiss a guy like that on the first date?"

She shrugged. "I don't know. I figured a peck on the cheek, like I give Grandpa, wasn't what he had in mind."

"I'm sure it wasn't. But Roarke was a jerk." He turned to face her again, his eyes prying deep inside of her. "Why don't you set your sights higher than guys like him and Robby?"

She had.

She was.

But her unrealistic crush on Blake would remain a secret and follow her to her grave.

"Maybe, if I knew how to kiss, I *would* set my sights higher."

The only sounds that filled the night air were crickets and bullfrogs calling to their mates.

An overwhelming urge to ask Blake to show her how to kiss began in her chest and radiated to the outer reaches of her body.

And deciding this might be her only chance, she asked, "Will you teach me how?"

Cindy's question hung in the air as the night grew alive with anticipation. And with sexual awareness.

Kiss Cindy?

Here, under a blanket of stars and a lover's moon? For a crazy moment, the idea held merit, and Blake was tempted to show her how a man and woman ought to kiss.

But then what?

He was a love-'em-and-leave-before-they-get-attached kind of guy. And for the life of him, he couldn't find the words to respond.

"What's one little kiss?" she asked, as though encouraged by his silence. "It's not like it has to mean anything."

No. It didn't. And he'd already told her that openmouthed kisses, at least when it came to her—and not his dates—was something that would evolve later, after she'd grown more comfortable with kissing. And with dating whoever she decided was good enough for her.

It must have been the spell of the full moon—that and the memories of their sensual slow dance filling his head—because Blake weakened, deciding to give in to her request.

He brushed his lips across hers, hoping to appease her—*and him, too,* if truth be told. Just touching the softness of her lips, catching the warmth of her breath, inhaling the fading hint of her peach-laced scent only made him yearn for more.

"That's not quite what I meant," she said. "That was pretty tame."

"You need to start out slow, lady. And you don't owe a guy squat just because he took you out. But for the record, that was a pretty decent thanks-for-the-date kind of kiss. And you did just fine."

"And what if the date was extra-special? And I want him to know that it had meant a lot to me. That *he* meant a lot to me, too."

"Well, then you deepen it a little."

"Deepen it?" she asked. "How? Do you mean open my mouth?"

"Not exactly." He didn't want her to open her mouth to just anyone.

"Then maybe I'd better try it again." She

smiled, as though the request was innocent enough.

So he brushed his lips against hers again, once, then twice, then a third time—the sensual yet tentative kind of kiss that a man gave a woman when he hoped she would take charge and make it more. Of course, that was just so Cindy could practice.

She turned in the swing, her thigh branding his, and wrapped her arms around his neck. Her breasts pressed lightly against his chest, reminding him that it was the new Cindy he was kissing.

This was just an opportunity for her to practice, he told himself as he slid his hands around her waist.

She leaned into him, her soft mouth pressed on his—unmoving. So he gave her a little nip with his lips, a gentle nudge. And she was soon kissing him back. Sweetly. Gently.

And then something happened, although, for the life of him, he wasn't sure what. But he got caught up in her scent, her touch, her taste. And the kiss deepened of its own accord. At least, that's what he told himself as his lips parted, parting hers, as well.

Their tongues touched, and the stars spun out of control. The night became magical, as

Cindy put her heart and soul into the kiss. He did, too. And he was completely lost.

She whimpered, and her hands threaded through his hair, pulling him closer. Deeper.

For a woman who claimed to be innocent, she certainly seemed to know what she was doing.

And for a man who ought to know better, he certainly didn't.

Heck, she'd wanted to practice kissing, not get a lesson in heavy petting.

Blake pulled back, breaking the kiss before he got carried away. Before he got any more carried away than he already had.

He raked a hand through his hair, not at all sure how he'd backpedal from this.

"I'm getting the hang of it," she said. "But I think I'll need one more lesson."

One more? She had to be kidding. There was no way he could kiss her again, not like that.

He'd even slipped his tongue into her mouth, after telling her not to let that happen on a first date.

Of course, this wasn't a date at all. But he suspected that only made it worse.

Either way, she'd had all the lessons she needed tonight.

He stood, and the swing shifted. So did his balance.

"Aren't you going to kiss me again?" she asked.

"Not on a moonlit night."

Then he strode out to the barn, leaving her alone on the porch while he tried desperately to ditch the effect she had on him.

Chapter Eight

Cindy wasn't sure why she continued to sit outside after Blake had walked away. Maybe because she feared her knees wouldn't be able to stand or make the trek into the house without buckling and causing her body to melt into a heap on the floor.

Never in her dreams had she imagined that Blake's kiss would make her head spin, her blood rush, her heart sing. And she had a feeling that Robby's kiss would fall short of the benchmark Blake had just set.

Robby would be back in town soon, if he wasn't home already. Would he give her a call, like he'd said he would?

A part of her, the place where her pride lurked, wished he would. But the part where her dreams lay dormant wasn't ready to face the man. Not until Blake had left town for good.

And taken his kisses with him.

Whew. She pushed back in the swing, letting it sway. She'd thought that one kiss would appease her curiosity and quench her dreams. But it hadn't. That star-spinning kiss had merely made her want more.

She listened to the late-night sounds—an occasional whinny in the pasture, the chirps of crickets, the croak of a bullfrog down by the creek.

It was well after midnight and past her bedtime. Shep, who'd gone inside with Grandpa, padded back through the living room, pressed his nose against the screen door and scanned the porch. He whimpered as though begging her to come inside for the night.

"I'm coming, boy. Just a little longer." She wasn't sure why she wanted to remain outside. Blake probably wouldn't come back this way until she went to bed, although she wasn't sure how she knew that.

The man had acted strangely, as though the kiss had knocked him out of his boots. And she sure hoped it had, even if it was silly and illogical for her to wish for something like that.

She studied the dark outline of the barn. Every now and then, she could see Blake's form. And she wondered what was going through his mind.

In the shadows near the corral, Blake waited for Cindy to go inside. He'd been struggling with his response to her arousing kiss.

He wasn't sure whether he was a great teacher or she was a fast learner. But as quickly as she'd caught on to the fine art of kissing, she could move to the head of the class.

If he closed his eyes, he could still feel her lips on his, seeking, tasting. Taunting.

He could still feel her breasts pressed against his chest, still hear her whimper as she ran her fingers through his hair. For Pete's sake, she'd nearly turned him inside out and hung him on the line to dry.

He'd told himself she was just a friend, just a girl he'd grown up with. But he wasn't looking at her that way anymore. He was attracted to her, more attracted than he cared to admit, and far more than was wise.

Of course, that didn't mean he'd string her

along or make any kind of commitment he couldn't keep.

He wandered around the barn, swung open the side door and hit the light switch, which cast a warm yellow glow inside. He checked Ariana, the roan mare, first. "Hey, girl. How are you doing?"

The mare snorted, as though telling him the last few weeks of gestation had been tough.

"It'll be over soon. Tuck and Cindy will take good care of you and that colt."

Then he made his way to the stall where Cutter rested for the night.

"I'm getting in too deep," he told the horse, his voice whisper soft. "Too close."

Cindy had him on edge. And it scared the liver out of him. If she were just another woman in town, and not Tuck's granddaughter, it wouldn't matter that much. Not that he'd want to break anyone's heart. But he'd be dipped if he would purposely hurt Cindy.

She needed so much more than a guy like him, a cowboy who didn't mind living in motels and moving from rodeo to rodeo.

Blake had found respect and acceptance on the circuit, and he wasn't going to give it up.

He *wouldn't* give it up. The rodeo was the only place he truly belonged.

"Let's go for a long ride tomorrow," he told the horse as he stroked the animal's neck. "Then we'll head out to the rodeo grounds. See if anyone else has shown up yet."

Cutter threw up his head as though nodding a yes.

"Sleep tight, buddy." Then Blake strode to the door, clicked off the light switch and walked outside. But he didn't step foot toward the house. Instead, he glanced at the porch, saw Cindy's shadowed figure on the swing, right where he'd left her.

He'd wait out here until she went inside. There was only so much pressure he wanted to put on his conscience. And tonight he'd reached his limit.

A couple of moments later, he heard the screen door squeak as she opened it. Then she went inside, leaving him to wrestle with the ghost of her presence, the memory of her scent, the warmth of her embrace.

Not to mention that blood-stirring, soul-searching kiss.

But instead of heading to bed himself, he leaned against the barn, rested his face against the outside wall and felt the cool wood siding on his cheek.

He couldn't stay on the Tumbling T much

longer. Cindy was doing something to him. Wearing him down. Making him vulnerable to God only knows what.

As far as he could see, there was only one option if he wanted to come out of this without hurting anyone.

He had to compete in the Blossom County Rodeo, then get the hell out of Dodge.

The next morning, after breakfast, Cindy poured herself one last cup of coffee. She didn't usually munch and snack between meals, but she'd been so eager to go to The Alibi last night that she'd yet to taste the pie she'd made. So, she cut a small sliver, placed it on a saucer and took a fork from the drawer. Then she dug into the crust, making sure she got a scoop of the apple filling.

Okay, so her pie didn't look too good, but surely it tasted better than it looked.

But...oh...ugh...yuck.

She was wrong. A wet salt lick rolled in sweetened wood shavings would have tasted better.

There was no way she could swallow, not without gagging, so she spit the nasty mouthful into the trash.

She had to give Blake credit. He'd managed

to get his bite down. And he hadn't complained, either.

He'd sidestepped the truth rather than hurt her feelings. And she appreciated his tact. But that didn't make her feel any better about being a lousy cook.

Last night, when she'd pulled the pie out of the oven, she'd figured that a couple of practice runs would improve the appearance of Aunt Millie's famous apple pie. But that was before she tasted the darn thing. And now she knew better.

So much for getting a blue ribbon for baking.

She dumped the rest of the pie into the sink and ran the garbage disposal. Maybe she ought to consider cooking lessons. She'd heard they offered a home economics class in the evening through the adult education department at the high school. But even if she drove to town and registered today, there wouldn't be enough time to hone her skills for this year's fair.

Had Cherry been mistaken?

The phone rang, jarring her from the depressing thoughts. When she answered, Susan Gray Feather introduced herself and asked to speak to Blake.

"He's out in the yard. If you'll hold on, I'll go get him for you."

"Thank you."

Cindy wished she had the guts to quiz the woman, to get to know her. To ask what she and Blake's father had done to hurt Blake as a child. But it wasn't her place.

She set the receiver on the counter and went looking for Blake. She found him in the barn, saddling Cutter.

"Your mother is on the phone."

He nodded, then finished adjusting the cinch. "Will you keep an eye on him for me?"

"Sure."

After a few minutes, he returned.

"Everything okay?" she asked.

"Yeah. My mom found a house and let me know how much she needed for the down payment. I'll mail her a cashier's check later this afternoon." He led the horse from the barn.

She couldn't help but ask, "Where are you going?"

"Nowhere in particular. Just for a ride."

There were a slew of things she ought to be doing, but none that seemed important. "Mind if I go, too?"

Blake had wanted to ride alone. But he supposed it didn't matter if Cindy went along. If they stayed on their respective mounts and didn't get within arm's length—or at least within kissing distance—it ought to be safe. "Sure, you can go with me."

"Thanks. Will you saddle a horse for me? The sorrel mare in the corral near the shed is one of my favorites. Her name is Foxy Lady, and her tack is next to Blackjack's, against the far wall in the barn." She flashed him one of the old Cindy smiles and tugged at the short skirt she wore. "Just give me a minute to change into something more appropriate."

Good. Her customary jeans and a cotton shirt would be better. Safer for him.

When she dashed into the house, he realized that when it came to getting dressed, her minutes were a lot longer than his these days. But it was too late. He'd already agreed to let her join him on a ride.

He saddled her horse, a two-year-old mare that had as much spunk as Cindy did.

Surprisingly, when he walked both horses to the front of the house, she bounded outside, smiling, eyes glimmering.

Where had she gotten those tight jeans that hugged her hips? Instead of one of those baggy plaid shirts she used to favor when riding, she'd chosen to wear one of the form-fitting T-shirts he'd bought for her at the Mercantile, although he couldn't remember it being so snug. There wasn't one blessed curve that didn't taunt him.

"I'm ready," she said as she took the reins from his hand.

He wasn't ready, but he wasn't sure how to tap-dance his way out of the ride now.

"Will you give me a boost?" she asked.

Just as he'd done many times in the past, he locked his fingers together, creating a make-shift step for her. And she lifted herself into the saddle, leather creaking, denim straining— hers and his.

As he mounted his own horse, he grumbled under his breath at the effect she was having on him. And if he didn't know better, he'd think she was trying to affect him on purpose.

"Come on," he said, his voice laced with exasperation he hadn't meant to reveal. "Let's go."

The sun rose high in the east, as a scatter of white, cotton-candy clouds dotted the Texas sky. It was a pretty summer morning, not too hot or humid—a perfect day for riding. A good day to enjoy the fresh air and God's handiwork in silence.

"It was nice of you to help your mother buy that house," Cindy said.

He didn't respond. Helping out his mom financially was just something he felt like doing. She'd made some positive changes in her life, and he supposed it was his way of supporting them.

"When was the last time you talked to your dad?" she asked, not getting the hint that he didn't want to chat right now, especially about his parents, his past.

"The last time I talked to him was over the phone. It was my eighth birthday."

"Why don't you look him up?"

Why would he want to do something like that? The man had bailed out on him years ago. "I figure, if he'd wanted to have any kind of relationship with me, he would have stayed in contact."

She nibbled on her lip as though stewing about something. But she didn't need to worry about him. He'd come to grips with his own reality long ago.

They didn't talk much after that, which suited him just fine.

As the horses rounded the bend, near Twin Oaks Lake, the best fishing spot in all of Blossom County, a couple of fishermen stood on the muddy shore, poles extended over the water.

Cindy used a hand to shade her eyes and

squinted. "Well, I'll be darned. One of those guys is Robby. I knew he was due home soon. And I should have expected him to come here first. He loves to fish."

She urged her mount forward, and Blake followed suit. He wanted to see the guy. Up close.

"Hey, Robby." She waved at the fishermen.

A tall, gangly young man wearing a green baseball cap turned his head, and when he recognized Cindy, a smile broke across his face. "Well, look at you."

Yeah. Just look at her.

She swung off her mount, all five-feet-nothing packed into a pair of tight-fitting jeans that made poor old Robby's jaw drop and eyes widen.

"I…uh…was meaning to call you," he said. "I meant to… I should have…called…as soon as I got home. But I…uh…well, I just didn't."

Blake got the feeling Robby was realizing he'd made a big mistake in not calling the moment he'd crossed the Blossom County line.

"I'm sure you had a lot of things to do." Cindy led the mare toward the shore. "I understand."

"Uh-huh." Robby's eyes never left her, and when he swallowed, his Adam's apple bobbled. "But I'm not busy anymore."

"Maybe we can go to a movie or something,"

she suggested, as though she was perfectly good at pickup lines and dating and didn't need Blake's help.

"Super. I'd like that." Robby looked at Blake, who remained mounted on Cutter. Watching. Assessing. And deciding the nerdy accountant was harmless. And smitten.

"This is Blake Gray Feather," Cindy said. "He and I practically grew up together although he'd already left home when your family moved to Blossom."

Was she implying that Robby had nothing to worry about? That Cindy and Blake could never be more than friends? Not that it mattered. But the casual brush-off niggled at him just the same.

"You're the famous bronc-buster." Robby smiled, revealing crooked front teeth. "Folks in town have been talking about you, calling you the Comanche Wonder."

Blake bristled. He'd never liked being separated from the crowd because of his bloodlines.

"Good luck in the rodeo competition," Robby said with a smile.

"Thanks."

"Oh." Robby glanced at the heavyset guy beside him. "This is my cousin, Brad. He's from

Houston. And he's waiting for word on the bar exam. He's going to be a lawyer."

Apparently, Robby was the kind of guy who measured a man's worth by his occupation, and Blake couldn't help wondering how cowboys measured up. Of course, if Robby had access to Blake's financial portfolio, he'd be more impressed.

Cindy flashed the almost-attorney a pretty smile. "It's nice to meet you, Brad. Are you guys having any luck catching anything?"

"Not yet."

Brad, who couldn't seem to take his eyes off Cindy, gave his cousin a goofy smile. "But it looks like Robby's luck is turning."

Apparently so.

Blake had always sympathized with nerdy guys like Robby, guys who didn't often fit in any better than he did, but he didn't like the idea of Robby dating Cindy.

An uneasiness—jealousy?—settled over him, making him sorry he'd sponsored her makeover. And sorry he'd let her tag along on his ride.

"How about dinner and a movie next Friday night?" Robby asked Cindy, before tossing a glance Blake's way, as though he needed permission or something.

She hooked her thumbs in the front pocket of her jeans, stretching the denim even tighter across her hips. "Friday's the chili cook-off at the Stampede, and Grandpa expects me to be there."

"Maybe Saturday?" the nerdy accountant asked.

"That's the first day of the rodeo," Cindy said. "But Thursday would work, if it's okay with you."

Robby broke into a thank-my-lucky-stars grin that probably wouldn't wash off, even if his attorney buddy got a wild hair and pushed him into the lake.

"Well," Cindy said, as she took a step back. "I guess we'd better get going. I'll see you on Thursday."

"Wonderful. I'll pick you up about six."

"Perfect." Then she reached for the saddle horn, lifted her foot—without any help from Blake—stuck the toe of her boot into the stirrup and swung that dynamite little shape onto her horse.

Robby's mouth gaped open, and Blake hoped the nerdy accountant caught a flying insect or two.

As they rode away, Cindy asked softly, "How did I do?"

"Like you damn sure don't need a coach any longer." He hadn't meant to snap like that. But it irritated the hell out of him to think of Cindy dating Robby. She could certainly do better than that.

Blake had an urge to take Robby aside and give him a man-to-man about how to treat Cindy. And to warn him not to even think of kissing her on the first date. "Come on. Let's head back to the ranch."

"Do you want to race?" she asked, a playful glimmer in her eyes.

Sure. Why not. The sooner he ended this ride and got back to the house, the better.

The new Cindy was about to drive him out of his mind.

And run off with his heart—if he was fool enough to let her.

Cindy knew she hadn't stood much chance of beating Blake in a horse race, although Foxy Lady had proved to be fast and sure on her feet. But it felt good to let the wind blow through her hair, to leave her worries behind.

She'd managed to snag a date with Robby and to appear happy about it. But if truth be told, she'd much rather be going to a movie and dinner with Blake on Thursday night.

But fat chance of that.

Once they neared the house, Blake pulled up, slowing to walk Cutter the rest of the way. Cindy came up beside him, the mare keeping pace with the chestnut gelding's stride.

When she was younger, she'd wondered how she would fare in rodeo competition, and at one time, she'd considered it. She had a natural talent on horseback that was every bit as good as Blake's.

But Grandpa needed her. He'd lost a wife, a son and a daughter-in-law in less than a year's time. And Cindy was the only family he had left. Taking off to ride on the circuit was out of the question.

As they rode into the yard, they noticed a sporty little red pickup parked in the driveway. And a tall, shapely blonde stood on the porch.

An attractive woman Cindy didn't recognize.

She wore a pair of new jeans and a white cotton blouse, but she wasn't dressed for a visit to a working horse ranch. Her clothing was western designer wear, no doubt, and she modeled it well.

The blonde hadn't yet noticed Blake and Cindy approach, when Shep sniffed at her lap. She grimaced and batted the dog away.

Tuck walked outside and handed her a glass of iced tea, smiling to beat the band.

"Who do you suppose that is?" Cindy asked, realizing Blake hadn't said much.

"Her name is Jessica Livingston."

Cindy's heart dropped to her gut. She didn't need to quiz him any further. He'd told her that *one in particular's* name was Jessica. And although Cindy wasn't surprised to see how pretty the young woman was, she hadn't expected her to be so…classy. So perfectly put together.

Shep barked at their approach, and Tuck waved.

Now it was too late to change direction, to lead Blake away from the woman who was obviously waiting for him and pleased to see him ride in.

Jessica set the glass of tea on the wicker table that rested near the porch swing, then strode to meet Blake, hips swaying, back straight, chin held high, a smile bursting forth. She carried herself like a woman who was comfortable with her femininity and knew just how to play the games men and women played. In fact, she was probably an ace.

A woman *so* not like Cindy.

"Surprised to see me?" the cowgirl asked the cowboy.

A grin tugged at Blake's mouth. "Yeah. As a matter of fact, I am."

Jessica glanced at Cindy and smiled, but those big blue eyes seemed to be sizing her up. And it irked Cindy to no end that she wanted to know what conclusion the pretty cowgirl had come to.

But she supposed it didn't matter. She'd never be able to compete with a woman like that.

Blake nodded his head at Cindy. "Jes, this is my friend, Cindy Tucker. We practically grew up together."

It had been the same thing Cindy had told Robby, but she'd been playing down her foolish attraction to her handsome riding companion. Blake was just stating a fact. And her pride took a tumble.

"Jessica is one of the top barrel racers in the country," Blake explained.

The blonde reached out an arm that sported a tennis bracelet. "Nice to meet you."

"Same here." Cindy reached down and shook Jessica's hand, forcing a smile that didn't come from the heart. She'd give it her best effort, but she didn't think she could sit here and pretend the reunion didn't bother her.

A powerful ache settled in her chest, and she blinked back the moisture building in her eyes. Like a voyeur, Cindy watched Blake dismount, watched the woman's eyes glimmer as if her arms were itching at the chance to give him a hug.

Was he as happy to see her as she was to see him?

Cindy could only study him, looking for a clue.

The leather creaked as Blake swung down from his horse. He wasn't particularly happy to see Jessica here. Not that he didn't like the woman. But her feelings ran stronger than his.

In an effort to downplay whatever had been going on between him and Cindy, he welcomed Jessica with a hug. "What brings you all the way out here?"

"You." She cast him a playful smile. "They say absence makes the heart grow fonder, and I wanted to know if that was true."

Blake glanced at Cindy, saw her taking it all in.

"I thought you might like to go with me to scout the rodeo grounds," Jessica said. "Maybe even show me around town, since this used to be your old stomping grounds."

"Sure. I'll need to cool down my horse. Can you wait?"

"Of course. I don't have anywhere to go."

Blake couldn't help glancing Cindy's way and catching the look on her face. A look that suggested she'd like nothing better than to suggest a place where Jessica could go.

Chapter Nine

Blake and Jessica had driven off in her sporty little pickup hours ago. And they'd yet to return.

Cindy couldn't help pacing the living room, couldn't help wondering where he was or what he was doing because, whatever it was, he was doing it with Jessica.

Why hadn't he called to let her and Grandpa know what time to expect him?

Okay. So Blake was an adult and could come and go as he pleased. But a little consideration, the kind afforded to roommates, would have been nice. And so would a call.

Of course, Grandpa had spent a lot of time

on the phone this afternoon—something he never did. He might chew a person's ear off in a face-to-face conversation, but, usually, he disliked chatting over the telephone.

Until this afternoon.

When he had finally hung up the receiver for the last time, he went down the hall toward his bedroom, whistling a jolly tune. And when he returned, fresh from the shower, he wore a pair of black jeans, a chambray shirt, his new boots and a subtle hint of Old Spice.

"Where are you going?" she asked.

"I've got me a date with the prettiest gal in all of Blossom County." A grin spread over his face, softening his timeworn skin, making him look about ten years younger. "Except for you, Cindy Lou."

She ought to feel touched by his compliment, but ever since that blond barrel-racer had shown up on the ranch, Cindy felt about as good-looking as a toad. "Are you going out with Loraine?"

"Yup. I'm taking her back to The Alibi. And this time, it'll be just the two of us." He took his hat from the peg near the front door and placed it on his head.

"This thing with Loraine sounds serious."

"Nope. It's pure fun." His eyes glimmered with amusement.

"That's not what I meant. I just thought that you planned to stay single for the rest of your life."

"I still might. I never gave the ladies much thought. Not until Loraine caught my eye. And now? I don't have any thoughts one way or the other about getting hitched. Yet. But I feel sort of renewed. Excited, you know? Like I've fallen into a time warp and I'm twenty-two again."

She tried to think of Grandpa as a man her age, but it was hard. Still, that's the way he was acting.

Your grandfather has the heart of a young man, Cherry had said. And that sure seemed to be true.

Funny thing, though. Cindy felt like an old lady. A spinster, to be exact. And the fact that she had a date with Robby on Thursday night didn't lift her mood in the least.

"Hey, little girl." Grandpa placed a callused finger under her chin and lifted her gaze to his. "What's the matter?"

"Nothing." She conjured a smile, willing it to reach her eyes.

"I don't believe that. Does it bother you that I've found a lady friend?"

"No. It just surprises me. That's all."

"That's *not* all. It's more than that, Cindy Lou. I know you. And your tail is dragging."

She never kept secrets from Grandpa. But what was she supposed to admit? That she'd fallen in love with a cowboy who was crazy about someone else, a pretty blonde who lived in his rodeo world? A cowgirl who was experienced in the ways of romance and flat-out sexier than any woman had a right to be.

"Everyone is going out tonight but me," she said, skating around the truth. "But don't worry. Shep and I will be just fine."

"Well, heck. You can come along with Loraine and I. We don't mind."

"Oh, no, I wouldn't think of it. I meant that I was sad I didn't have my own date."

"The right man will come along one day, and you'll break free of me and this ranch and start a life of your own." He placed a kiss on her brow. "Don't wait up for me."

"I won't," she told him, but she wasn't going to sleep a wink tonight.

Not until her heart stopped aching.

At a quarter to eight, Jessica brought Blake back to the ranch.

Her hands rested on the steering wheel,

her eyes trained on him. "Do you want me to wait?"

"No. I don't need any help and I don't need a ride. I've got my truck."

"All right," she said. "Then I'll head back to the motel."

He reached for the door handle and slid from the Ford Ranger pickup.

"You know," she added. "You didn't need to get your own room. You could have shared mine."

"I know." As appealing as her offer might have been at one time, Blake had no desire to share anything with Jessica. "Like I told you before, I'm not ready to jump back into a relationship."

"I know, but I'm willing to wait." She flashed him a weighted smile. "For a while."

He nodded, closed the passenger door, then headed for the house as Jessica drove away.

Tuck's truck was no longer parked beside the barn, so Blake wasn't sure if anyone was home, in spite of the lamp that burned softly in the living room. He reached into his pocket for his key. But he didn't need one. The door was open.

He entered the house and found Cindy standing near the sofa, a paperback novel resting on the end table.

She wore a white cotton nightgown and had swept her hair into a topknot. Loose, wispy curls framed her face and made her too darn pretty for words. She looked fresh from the shower and ready for bed.

He caught a whiff of the aloe soap that she kept in the bathroom. He liked the scent—on her, anyway.

Just looking at her standing there, like a goodhearted woman waiting at home for a two-timing man, made his heart go haywire.

She offered him a hesitant smile. "You're home."

No. Not really. He'd just come to pack his bag, but for a moment, it almost felt as though he had come home. To her.

And *that*, if anything, convinced him he was doing the right thing. "I...uh...came to get my stuff. I'm going to stay in town so I'll be closer to the rodeo grounds."

It sounded like a lame excuse, even to him, but he had to put some distance between him and Cindy.

How else could he still those sappy urges he'd been having? Urges he continued to have, just seeing her greet him by the door wearing only her nightgown.

The lamplight played havoc with his senses,

as it shone through the worn cotton, making the gown nearly see-through and drawing his eyes to the silhouette of her body. He figured she didn't have a clue how seductive she looked, how revealing the gown was with the light at her back. And rebel that he was, he wouldn't tell her she ought to put on a robe.

She crossed her arms, hiding the hint of her breasts from his view. "I don't think it's the rodeo that made you pack your bags. It's Jessica."

He didn't have the guts to tell her she was wrong, that it was *her* who had him all stirred up and not knowing which way to run. "I've got a lot of friends arriving in town. And I need to focus on the rodeo, check out my competition."

Then he excused himself and disappeared into his room.

Cindy wanted desperately to buy Blake's explanation even though, in her heart, she had her doubts. She might be new at the romance game, but she had Jessica figured out. The woman wanted Blake.

But did he want her?

Maybe so. But that heated kiss he and Cindy had shared had been special. And it had shaken her to the core. Him, too, she suspected.

Blake was packed and heading for the door when a sudden realization struck. This might be her last chance to remind him of the kiss. To discuss what could have...what might have...

"Wait." She reached for his forearm. "I need to ask you something."

He paused, his eyes asking, *What?*

"That kiss we shared on the porch last night touched you, too. Didn't it?"

For the longest time, he stood there, staring at her. Reality cutting through the bull.

"Yeah," he said, his voice a whisper-soft caress. "The kiss rocked."

A thrill of excitement shot clean through her, jump-starting her hopes and dreams.

If the kiss had moved him, then maybe he felt something more for her than friendly affection. Maybe he even loved her a little. But if she didn't ask, she might never know. "Does that mean you care about me? More than you thought?"

He stood stone-cold silent for the longest time, as though struggling to answer truthfully yet tactfully. "Yeah. I care for you. More than I thought."

It wasn't an admission of love. But it felt awfully darn close to her and might be as much as she'd ever get from him. If she could believe he loved her, it would be enough. It would have to be.

"Do you care about me in a romantic sense?" she asked.

Again the silence nearly roared in her ears, her mind, her heart.

"I don't kiss my friends the way I kissed you." He wrestled with the handle of his canvas tote bag, although his paw-in-a-steel-trap expression suggested that he was grappling with a whole lot more than that. "But that's as far as it'll ever go, Cindy. I'm not the kind of man you should waste your love on."

Then he brushed a brotherly kiss across her brow and headed for the door.

She was too stunned to speak. Too taken aback to think of a response, an argument. A plea.

And now it was she who stood silent, immobile.

Blake walked out of the house and shut the door. And when he was gone, the thrill of his admission disappeared. Her shoulders slumped, and she nearly dropped to the floor, heartbroken and defeated.

She'd just lost the man she loved, the man who might love her a little in return.

And there didn't seem to be anything she

could do about it except throw herself at his feet and beg.

But she wouldn't do that.

Instead, she stood in the middle of the room, an ache as big as Texas in her heart and tears spilling down her cheeks.

Cindy hadn't slept at all that night. She'd tossed and turned like a trout that had detoured into a shallow stream.

Grandpa had come home after two, but she'd remained in bed, listening to him tiptoe down the hall while whistling that same happy tune. It was nearly dawn when she'd finally fallen asleep, and she didn't wake until nearly ten.

After a shower, she prepared a fresh pot of coffee and watched it perk, inhaling the rich aroma and hoping the smell alone would provide a lift.

She felt defeated. Stuck. And for the life of her, she couldn't think of anything to do that would change things.

The telephone rang, and she snatched the receiver on the second ring. "Hello?"

"I'm sorry for bothering you again," Susan Gray Feather said. "But can I please speak to Blake?"

"He's not here." Cindy wasn't sure if she

should offer to take a message. She couldn't go chasing after Blake, especially when she suspected he had Jessica glued to his hip. And she wasn't sure when—or if—he'd come back to the ranch. "He's gone into town to be close to the rodeo grounds. I can try to get a message to him."

"It's not important. I just wanted to let him know the cashier's check he overnighted to me arrived and the house is mine." She paused. "And I wanted to thank him again for helping me, especially since...well, you know, all the trouble we had in the past."

No, Cindy didn't know. Not really. Blake had always kept his feelings pretty close to the vest. But she couldn't help prodding the woman to speak. "I'm sure there are two sides to every story."

"Most of what Blake has told you is probably true," Blake's mom added. "I was a miserable woman while he was growing up. And a closet drinker. But I joined AA and I've been sober for three years now. In retrospect, I realize how difficult I made things for him while he lived with me."

"Blake said your relationship is better now," Cindy said.

"That's true. But things are still strained between us. And I'd do anything in the world to make it up to him—if he'd give me a chance. I'd even go looking for my ex-husband, if I thought it would help."

"Why do you think finding Blake's father would make a difference?"

"Clint and I had more than our share of disagreements, but he was a good father and loved his son. And Blake loved him, too. He used to tag after his dad all the time. In fact, Blake was more Clint's child than mine. And I was often jealous of their relationship." She blew out a slow and steady sigh, as though the memory had been held in secret for too long. "When Clint left me, I was crushed. I wanted to hurt him as badly as he hurt me. But it was Blake who was hurt the most."

Those were the wounds Cherry had been talking about, Cindy realized. The wounds only Blake could heal.

"I let him believe his father didn't want anything to do with us. But it was me the man left, *me* he wanted to avoid."

"Blake's father could have taken you to court and sued for visitation," Cindy said, not wanting the woman to carry all of the blame.

"Yes, and to make sure he couldn't do that, I

moved out of state and didn't leave a forwarding address."

"Do you know where his father is now?" Cindy asked.

"Oklahoma, I think. He had family who lived there and had always talked about moving back. I could call my ex-sister-in-law."

"That sounds like a good start to me." Maybe meeting his father would be the first step in Blake's healing process.

"Thanks for listening to me ramble," the woman said. "It's not always easy to talk to Blake."

No it wasn't.

When the line disconnected, Cindy poured herself a cup of coffee and grieved for the little boy who'd felt abandoned by a man who hadn't willingly left him. A child who hadn't felt loved while growing up.

But Cindy loved him. Deeply.

She probably understood him better than anyone. No one knew how badly he needed a family of his own to love. A place where he truly belonged.

And Cindy was more than willing to create that place with him. If he'd let her.

She wouldn't give up on him. Or on them.

Not without a fight.

Thirty minutes later, she'd dressed in one of the sexier outfits Blake had purchased for her—the black dress she'd worn to The Alibi. The one that had left him unsettled and bothered. And feeling a little possessive.

After taking extra care with her hair and makeup, she drove out to the rodeo grounds in search of the man she loved.

She parked near the entrance. As she climbed from the truck, a willowy blonde got out of the car parked in the next space.

It was Elizabeth Dupres.

Cindy had always considered Elizabeth a friend, even though they'd never really socialized.

"Hi, Cindy." Elizabeth offered her a friendly smile. "I like your new hairdo. I heard you'd had it styled at the Cut N Curl. It's really pretty."

"Thanks. What brings you to the fairgrounds?" Cindy asked.

Elizabeth's mother, Bitsy Dupres, was one of the more outspoken members of the Committee for Moral Behavior. Elizabeth, who taught first grade, was a member of the committee, too. But not nearly as vocal.

"The CMB has always been very supportive of the fair and the exhibits," Elizabeth explained. "It's just the carnival that we're concerned about. And its effect on the children in the community."

"What's going on today?" Cindy asked. "The fair hasn't opened yet."

"I'm going to help set up the children's art exhibit. And I'll be judging the youth photography entries."

That didn't surprise Cindy. Elizabeth had always been involved in the community. She was a thoughtful and considerate young woman, the kind of woman Cindy would like to have as a friend.

"I'm heading over to the rodeo grounds to talk to Blake," Cindy said. "But maybe later, some other day, if you have time, we could meet in town for lunch or something."

Elizabeth flashed her a pretty smile. "I'd love to have lunch with you. I have a lot more time on my hands during the summer. Maybe tomorrow at the Bee Hive diner?"

"That sounds great. Should we meet there at noon?"

"That works for me." Elizabeth motioned toward the hall that housed the home and hobby exhibits. "I'd better get over there. They're expecting me."

Cindy nodded, then proceeded on her way. Making a lunch date with a friend had been so easy that she wasn't sure why she hadn't done it sooner. Just knowing she had reached out to Elizabeth put a little bounce in her walk.

She hoped having a friend who was a member of the committee wouldn't mean the group would try to recruit her. She'd always loved the carnival. And she wouldn't think of joining a boycott.

But Elizabeth Dupres wasn't the kind to pressure anyone.

As Cindy crossed the grassy field that separated the rodeo arena from the fairgrounds, an older cowboy swaggered toward her. She wasn't sure where he'd come from—the beige fifth-wheel trailer parked near the fair office, she supposed.

The forty-something cowboy gave her a hard-to-read smile and lifted a sweat-stained straw hat. "Hi there, pretty lady."

She could smell alcohol and tobacco on his breath, and her instinct told her to avoid him. But she didn't want to be rude. "Hello."

"Can I escort you somewhere?"

"No, I'm just looking for a friend."

"If you don't find him or her, I'd be happy to step in." He flashed her another grin, then scanned the length of her with an appreciative eye. "That's a mighty fine-looking dress you're wearing. And you've got just about the prettiest hair I ever did see. It's the color of autumn leaves."

"Thank you." She couldn't help but return his smile. Nor could she suppress a surge of feminine power.

He reached for a strand of her hair and fingered it with a dirty, callused hand. "Why don't we go back to my trailer and have us a little drink?"

He'd had a few too many drinks already. And she wasn't the least bit interested in going to his trailer. The uneasiness she'd felt earlier returned in a steady rush.

"I have someplace to go." She stepped back and veered to the left, intending to walk around him.

He placed a hand on her shoulder. "Now, don't start playing hard to get."

"I'm not playing." She jerked away and walked toward the arena with quick and steady strides.

"You're a tease," he hollered behind her. "Do you know that?"

She didn't know anything, other than that she'd attracted the attention of the wrong man.

The only man she wanted to notice her was Blake.

Where was he?

* * *

Near the arena, Blake tipped back an ice-cold bottle of water, gulping down the refreshing drink. He'd pitched in and helped Trent Holbrook stack a truckload of alfalfa, because Hank Navarro, the guy who lived in a trailer near the fair office and was in charge of the Blossom County Rodeo, had started hitting the bottle this morning for some crazy reason. And he "just plumb forgot" to line up someone to unload the truck. And since Hank, who was a heck of a nice guy when he was sober, was in no shape to climb on a stack himself today, Blake had volunteered.

And he was glad he did.

The physical exertion helped him to forget—for a while, anyway—the look in Cindy's eyes when he'd left her last night.

But he'd had to let her go. And it was tough—as tough as having to put down a favorite old horse he didn't want to suffer.

Of course, that didn't mean she wasn't on his mind. Or that he'd managed to loosen the hold she had on his heart.

Man. He blew out a sigh. It was hot today. Humid.

He'd shed his shirt after unloading the hay

and draped it over the railing of the corral he was leaning against.

As he finished the last of his water, quenching his thirst, Jessica walked up and stood beside him. "I never knew a man who looked as good bare-chested as you do."

"Maybe you haven't been looking hard enough."

"I'm not ready to move on."

More than a few buddies had told him he was crazy for not taking what she was offering. But the truth was, that stupid kiss he'd shared with Cindy had done something to him. To his conscience.

And he didn't think he'd be able to shake it for a long time.

He lifted his hat, swiped the back of his hand at the sweat that gathered on his brow and scanned the area that would soon be a busy midway. From what he'd already gathered, the Committee for Moral Behavior, or better known in town as the CMB, hadn't admitted defeat. And he sensed trouble on the horizon. Of course, he wasn't about to get involved, but if he had to take sides, he sympathized with the carnies, who didn't fit in to the community of Blossom any better than he did.

As his attention drifted to the field that separated the rodeo arena from the fair grounds, he spotted a familiar redhead coming his way. She was sporting the little black dress that had driven him nuts at The Alibi. And it was doing a real number on him now.

She was crossing the field that separated the arena from the fairgrounds, heading this way.

And when their eyes met, his heart thudded in his chest like a piston that was about to blow.

She stopped her momentum, as though wanting to change direction. A moment later, she proceeded toward him again, her steps tentative. Slow. But she was closing the gap between them.

Until Jessica ran a possessive hand along his back, stood on tiptoe and pressed a kiss on his cheek.

Then Cindy stopped dead in her tracks.

Chapter Ten

The moment Cindy saw Jessica kiss Blake, her soaring heart took a tumble and belly flopped, right into the pit of her stomach. She couldn't believe she'd driven all the way out to the rodeo grounds to talk to him, to bare her heart and soul.

What kind of fool would chase after a man who didn't want her?

And even if he cared about her, like he'd said, Cindy couldn't compete with a woman like Jessica. Why, just look at her, with that saucy smile and those tight-fitting jeans. And she was hanging all over him.

So what was Cindy supposed to do now? She

couldn't very well stand planted in the middle of the grassy field like a dumbstruck scarecrow. But neither could she say all the things she'd been rehearsing: I love you, Blake—always have, always will.

Sheesh.

Of course, she could tuck her tail between her legs, turn around, head for the truck and skedaddle back to the ranch, as her dreams tagged behind in a cloud of dust. But then she'd look pathetic, as well as stupid.

Okay. Think. Surely she could come up with a good reason for getting all dressed up and driving out here.

Hey. She could tell him his mother had called, and thinking that it might be important, Cindy had hurried out to let him know.

All right, maybe it wasn't a flash of brilliance. But it was the best she could come up with at the moment.

So she continued toward him—toward them—putting one foot in front of the other, trying not to let her spiked heels sink too deep in the soft soil that lay beneath the lawn.

Blake hadn't moved from his spot against the railing. And neither had Jessica.

Cindy's steps didn't falter, but her resolve did. Maybe she *shouldn't* make an excuse for coming to talk to him. She'd kept her feelings a secret for too darn long. Why not toss the ball into his court and see what happened?

Telling him how she felt might put a strain on their friendship and make him uncomfortable to come around the ranch. But so what? She'd be dying inside whenever he did show up, especially if he had another woman on his arm—Jessica or someone like her.

Of course, there was always the chance that putting her heart on the line might make a difference. That it might make him reevaluate how he felt.

He'd said he wasn't the kind of man Cindy should waste her love on, but it was too late. She already loved him so much she could pop a button while shouting it out in the middle of the town square.

But knowing that he merely *cared* for her weighed on her mind, slowing her steps.

Should she still tell him how she felt? Risk the vulnerability?

She wasn't sure, but keeping her love a secret was killing her. So she sucked up all the self-confidence she'd built since that day he'd taken her to the Cut N Curl and, armed with all the courage she could muster, marched toward the arena. She didn't know what she'd say, how she'd approach it. But this was going to be a day of reckoning.

When she reached the couple, Jessica's arm slid low on Blake's back. Her fingers dropped to his belt, lingering on his denim-covered backside in a sensually possessive way.

Blake stepped to the side, breaking contact with the blonde—or so it seemed.

Cindy crossed her arms and shifted her weight to one foot. "Blake, can I speak to you for a minute?"

Jessica didn't seem to get the hint.

"Alone," Cindy added.

A normal woman would have excused herself. Would have considered that Cindy and Blake might want a private conversation. But not Jessica. She still didn't budge.

It had been years since Cindy's last playground fight. And she suspected most grown women didn't resort to slapping, scratching and hair pulling, like they did when they were girls. Of course, she'd learned early on that a good, swift sock in the nose would usually put a stop to the girly fights pretty darn quick. Either way, as long as she didn't have to compete in a beauty contest or a talent show with Jessica, the woman didn't scare her a bit.

But maybe Jessica was afraid of Cindy, afraid to let her speak to Blake alone.

If so, that was a first.

"Jes," Blake said. "Go find something to do, will you?"

"Sure." The cowgirl eyed Cindy before leaving. And as she walked away, her hips swayed and her blond hair swished over her shoulders.

"Sorry about that." Blake nodded toward the direction Jessica had taken but didn't give her retreating form a second glance. "The more I pull away from her, the more she dogs my steps. I guess she's not used to having a man turn down her affection."

"Maybe you need to be more direct," Cindy said. "You sure didn't put a stop to that kiss or the back rub."

Blake wasn't sure how much clearer he could be. He wasn't looking to settle down. And if he were...

His gaze met Cindy's. "What brings you out here?"

She uncrossed her arms, shifted her weight and tucked a strand of hair behind her ear. "There's something I need to tell you."

"What's that?" He stood up straight and pushed away from the railing. "Is Tuck okay?"

"Grandpa couldn't be better. Or happier. He

went out last night and didn't get in until two in the morning."

"You came all the way out here to tell me that?"

"No, I drove all the way out here to tell you that I love you."

Her admission slammed into him like a bronc out of the chute. And even though he found it more than a little exhilarating, it scared the hell out of him, too.

She placed her hands on her hips in a sexy, sultry way, then nibbled on her bottom lip and gazed at him with expressive green eyes that shimmered with innocence, sincerity and all the things a man wanted in a woman. A wife.

"I've always had this secret crush on you," she admitted. "But ever since you came back to town, I began to realize that what I felt was much bigger, much stronger than a crush."

His heart swelled, sputtered and did all kinds of crazy things, like banging against his chest wall and begging for mercy. The thought of Cindy's unabashed love terrified him. "I don't know what to say."

"You can start by telling me that you care enough about me to give us a chance."

"Ah, Cindy. I care a lot about you. Enough to refuse to give us a chance."

"I don't understand."

"I'm a rodeo cowboy. It's what I do. It's who I am."

"I know how much the rodeo means to you, and I'd travel the circuit with you, if you loved me, too." She made it all sound so easy, but it was far more complex than that.

He struggled to find an argument she could understand.

"Do you love me?" she asked, her voice soft yet pinning him down, making it hard to breathe. "Even just a little?"

More than anything in the world, he wanted to lie to her. To tell her he didn't love, didn't need, anyone. After all, he'd been telling himself that ever since he was a kid. But he couldn't lie.

He hadn't wanted to admit what was happening between them—and he still wasn't sure what was going on in his heart—but he wasn't the kind of man who could settle down and become part of the community. And if he were, he wasn't sure he'd even want to.

Obviously, Cindy took his silence as a no. She nodded toward the paddocks, where Jessica waited for him. "Is it because of her?"

"No. It's not about her at all."

"I could understand if it was."

Blake took her face in his hands. His thumbs

caressed the silky skin of her cheeks. His eyes locked on hers. "You're every bit as pretty as Jessica. And a heck of a lot more appealing. It's not *her*. It's me. I don't belong here in Blossom. And you don't belong on the road. You have a home and a family with Tuck. And that's why I'm not the man for you. No matter what either of us feels."

"You belong here." She placed a hand on her heart. "With me."

Cindy would never know how badly he wanted to take her up on the offer, how he wished he could throw caution to the wind and risk hurting her in the future. But he couldn't. "Honey, next time you're in town, listen to the people taking sides on the carnival issue. Count how many of them are trying to block the outsiders from moving in."

"It's not the same."

"In a way, it is. You've offered me something sweet, something special, something I have no right accepting. I'm honored. But you need to go home. I can't give you what you deserve." Then he dropped his hands, dismissing her from his life. From his heart. And he wondered if her disappointment matched his own.

Her lips quivered, and she blinked glossy eyes. "Then, I guess, there's nothing more to say." As she turned to go, she stopped. "Oh. I forgot to tell you. Your mother called this morning. She bought the house and wanted to thank you."

The sound of Cindy's voice, soft, ragged and bruised, about did him in. "My mom doesn't need to keep thanking me. It was no big deal."

She shrugged. "Maybe not, but she needs to talk to you about something else. I don't think she was honest with you about your father."

"What do you mean?"

"She said it was her fault he didn't come around. Maybe you'd better talk to her."

"I'll give her a call this evening. Thanks."

Then he watched as she turned and walked away, her head held high, those heels wobbling a little in the grass. And he almost chased after her.

Almost, but not quite.

He'd done the right thing, even though something clawed at his chest, trying to get out. And like a masochist, intent on suffering, he stood for a moment longer and watched her go.

There was nothing for Cindy to do but leave. She couldn't very well throw herself at his boots and beg.

She glanced one last time over her shoulder toward the paddocks, where Jessica stood, wearing a smug look on her face.

Cindy could have sworn she heard a small voice whisper, "Loser."

Loser.

That was about the size of it.

Cherry had predicted Cindy would be a winner at the fair, but the psychic obviously had been mistaken. Cindy wasn't going to win squat. Not a blue ribbon for pie baking, that was for sure. And she certainly hadn't snagged Blake away from Jessica.

Blake might have told the woman he wasn't interested in her, but Jessica's persistence was bound to win out. She'd get the man she'd set her sights on. And just the thought of that woman—or any other—embracing Blake, kissing him, hurt like the dickens.

As she neared the fairgrounds, she choked back a sob and swiped at the tears that trickled down her cheeks. And she cursed them under her breath. She'd never been a crybaby. Of course, she'd never been brokenhearted before.

"Hey there, little lady." The cowboy who'd stopped her earlier stood up from one of the lawn chairs that rested under his trailer awning and made his way toward her.

She felt like telling him to take a hike, to

mind his own business—whatever that might be—but she didn't trust her voice to come out with much authority. Not while the pieces of her heart were clogging her throat.

"You don't look so busy now. In fact, you look like someone kicked your dog." He opened his arms and eased closer to her. "How about a little hug to make you feel better."

"Thanks anyway, but I don't need a hug." She cleared her throat and brushed at another onset of tears.

"Did somebody make you cry? Maybe one of those rodeo cowboys? That ain't no way to treat a lady." He shot her a crooked grin. "But I got me the perfect cure for what ails you."

When he placed a meaty hand on her shoulder, she came to her rope's end. Hurt, frustrated and still feeling as though she ought to clobber someone or something, she doubled her fist and let loose with all she had, socking him square in the nose.

"Aaaagh!"

Blood burst forth like a spigot, and he looked up at her, clearly mystified. "What'd ya go and do that for?"

"Keep your hands to yourself. I told you I didn't need a hug."

The sound of a holler took Blake by complete surprise. He turned from one last I'm-not-interested discussion with Jessica, which was far more direct than any they'd had in the past, and spotted Cindy standing next to Hank Navarro, the head honcho of the Blossom County Rodeo.

The old cowboy could be a hellion when he drank. And to make matters worse, he'd gotten a wild hair and started drinking Jack Daniel's right after breakfast.

Hank moaned and bellowed, a hand held over his nose, bright red blood seeping through his fingers.

Cindy held fisted hands on her hips, as if she were ready to go head-to-head with him—again. And although she appeared to have held her own, Blake took off at a run and was beside them in nothing flat.

The best Blake could figure, Hank had offended her. "What's going on?"

"That crazy woman hit me," Hank roared, displaying the alcohol-induced meanness Blake had heard about. "She just went nuts and let me have it with a right hook."

"She didn't hit you for no reason," Blake said.

"The heck she didn't. I was just trying to be nice and she…" Hank removed his hand, looked at the bloody palm side and snarled. "Damn. I think she busted my nose. I ought to call the sheriff and have her arrested for assault."

"You go right ahead," Blake said. "Sheriff McCabe is an old friend of mine."

"And I'll tell the sheriff you accosted me." Cindy lifted her fist. "If you touch me again when I tell you not to, I'll blacken your eye."

Blake might be getting on Hank's bad side, but it didn't matter. He wasn't going to let anyone manhandle Cindy and get away with it even though, judging by the way Hank's nose was bleeding, the drunken cowboy hadn't gotten away with anything.

But that didn't make Blake feel any less protective toward the tomboy-turned-lady. So he stepped around, facing Cindy, and took her shoulders in his hands. "Are you okay, honey?"

She nodded.

"Hell, Gray Feather," Hank said. "I didn't realize she was your woman."

His woman?

Was that who Cindy was?

He looked at Hank, then returned his gaze to Cindy, saw the golden highlights in her red hair, the spring-green eyes that held more emotion than he'd allowed himself to feel in years.

The pesky little girl who'd become his friend

had grown up to be a woman who was so much more than a pretty face.

The old and new Cindys merged into one irresistible package—a package he wanted to honor and protect for the rest of his life, a woman he would cherish.

Something powerful snaked around his sorry heart, filling it to the bursting point and refusing to let go.

He loved her. It was as simple as that. And a sense of pride surged clean through him. "Yeah, Hank. She's mine. All five-feet-nothing of beauty, sass and spunk."

Cindy reached up and caressed his cheek, her fingers lingering on his jaw. "I'm not sure what got into you, but I'd like to bottle it and save it for a rainy day."

He slipped his arms around her. "You don't have to bottle it, honey. You're going to get a lifetime supply."

"Does that mean you love me?" she asked, eyes wide with expectation. Longing. Love.

The depth of her emotion—his, too—shook him to the core. "I don't know why it took me so long to see it, to admit it, but I love you Cindy Lou Tucker."

She raised up on tiptoe and threw her arms around his neck, eyes reaching deep into his heart and giving it a powerful squeeze. "I love you, Blake Gray Feather. I always have and always will. And just in case there's any doubt, I know how much the rodeo means to you. And I'm willing to follow the circuit or go to Timbuktu, as long as I can be with you."

Sometimes a loner had to find a place where he belonged. And right now, there was no doubt in Blake's mind that he belonged with Cindy.

Then he kissed her with all the love in his heart. A kiss that spoke of white lace and a happy-ever-after.

As his tongue swept the inside of her sweet, peppermint-laced mouth, claiming her for now and always, she whimpered, drawing him closer. Deeper. Giving, taking.

Blake had been running from home, family and love for years. But this time, he wasn't going anywhere. He was accepting all that Cindy offered him—the hand and the heart of the prettiest woman in Texas. And he was giving her his heart, too. Every inch of it, even the parts that had been wounded once upon a time.

When they finally came up for air, when the earth-spinning, knee-buckling kiss ended, Cindy flashed him a smile that branded his heart.

A grin tugged at his lips. "I don't suppose you'll mind canceling your date with Robby. I'm not going to share you."

"No problem," Cindy said, eyes glimmering. "I'll talk to him as soon as I get home."

"Good. I'll drive. We can leave your truck here for the time being." He released his embrace, took her by the hand and led her toward the parking lot where she'd left the truck. "And while you're telling Robby that you're taken, I'll officially ask Tuck for your hand."

"You want to marry me?" she asked, eyes wide with disbelief and happiness.

"If you'll have me."

"In a heartbeat." She tugged on his hand, pulling him to a stop, then wrapped her arms around him and convinced him with her kiss.

As far as the carnival issue, the line was still deeply drawn through the town of Blossom, with each citizen having one opinion or the other. But that didn't mean the community was down on the fair altogether. No way.

Ever since the founding fathers had planned the very first exposition, folks had come from miles around to marvel at the vast array of exhibits and eat their fill of epicurean delights, such as foot-long hot dogs, cotton candy and, more recently, deep-fried Twinkies.

For months the townspeople had been pumped and braced to enter the multitude of competitions that took place year after year, like the diaper derby, the pie-eating contest and the tractor pull.

And now the fair would start in less than a week.

On Friday afternoon, just after one o'clock, Blake and Cindy drove out to the fairgrounds for the stampede, which would kick off the rodeo that was scheduled to start Saturday and run through Monday night. They pulled into the parking lot, just behind Grandpa and Loraine.

Cindy liked the woman her grandfather was dating—and not just because Loraine had a great sense of humor, was a whiz in the kitchen and had promised to give Cindy cooking lessons. But the blond nurse seemed to adore Grandpa, and the old cowboy had never seemed happier.

"Do you think he's in love with Loraine?" Cindy asked Blake.

"Looks like it to me." He slid her a crooked grin. "And I know a cowboy in love when I see one."

"When's the last time you saw a cowboy in love?"

"This morning when I shaved."

Cindy, who sat in the middle of the cab next to the man she loved, bumped her shoulder against his. "I hope that cowboy looks at you every morning."

"I'm sure he will."

Cindy had no idea that falling in love would be like this. Stolen kisses. Heartfelt glances that spoke of forever. And she wished everyone could find what she'd found with Blake.

Grandpa had been thrilled to hear that Blake and Cindy planned to get married and wasn't the least bit disappointed to find out that she was going to leave home and join Blake on the rodeo circuit. But when she announced her intention to compete and join the Professional Rodeo Cowboy Association, he practically danced a jig.

There had never been any question about Cindy having the talent, but now she had the desire. And the first thing she planned to do, once she was eligible to compete as a pro, was to show Jessica a thing or two about barrel racing.

"It looks like Tuck and Loraine beat us here," Blake said as he parked the dual-wheeled truck in a stall next to Grandpa's pickup.

The older couple had no more than climbed from their vehicle when Blake shut off the engine and opened his door.

"Better get a move on," Grandpa said, as he took Loraine's hand and led her toward the booths that hosted the chili cook-off. "I'll have all of Carl Walburn's World-Famous Gut-Rot Chili gone before you can shake a stick at me."

Blake laughed. "You go on ahead. I've always been partial to Louella Swandale's Fire-Eater's Delight."

"See you two later," Loraine said over her shoulder, as she hurried to keep up with Grandpa's pace.

"We'll save you a seat at the concert," Cindy called after her.

Following the cook-off, several local country-western bands would be hitting the stage just after dark. Both couples looked forward to sitting beneath a silvery moon—spooning, according to Grandpa—and listening to the concert on the green.

As Blake and Cindy strolled along the lawn, hand in hand, they weren't in a hurry to reach the rodeo grounds. It was enough to be together, to face the future with anticipation.

"Well, look who's here," Blake said, nodding toward Cherry Cooper, who was scanning the area where the midway would soon be set up. "It's Lady Pandora."

"Let's say hello." Cindy drew him toward the fortune-teller, who seemed to blend in with members of the community in a pair of jeans. But a blouse made of colorful scarves hinted at the uniqueness of her talent and her profession.

"Hi, Cherry. Are you going to the stampede?" Cindy asked.

"No, I'm afraid not. I'm meeting Carlo Fuentes and the rest of the carnival people here. While waiting, I was checking out the area where the midway will be."

The fair and carnival would open on Wednesday, which meant there was probably a ton of prep work that needed to be done.

Cindy smiled at Cherry, admiring the woman's taste in clothes. "That's a pretty blouse."

"Thank you." The attractive brunette grinned. "You're looking lovely, too. And with that handsome cowboy at your side, you've got a glow to you. One that will shine a lifetime."

Cindy bumped Blake's elbow with her arm. "Cherry predicted I would be a winner and shine at the fair. And she was right."

"Well, you won my heart," he said. "That ought to count for something."

"It sure does. And you were skeptical."

"He still is," Cherry said. "I can see it in his eyes. And that surprises me, especially with his Comanche heritage and culture."

"I've never been one to chase after my Indian roots," Blake said.

Cherry batted a flyaway curl from her cheek. "It's time you did."

He shrugged. "Maybe so. I talked to my mother last night, and she's trying to find my father's family."

The psychic reached out and touched Blake's arm.

Was she trying to get a reading?

She closed her eyes momentarily. When she opened them, she smiled. "She'll find your father in Oklahoma. He's eager to meet you."

"I hope you're right," Blake said. "Deep inside, I always wondered if he was as bad as my mom had made him out to be. But I never wanted to get my hopes up or set myself up for more disappointment. After all, he ran off and never looked back."

"Your father has been looking for you for a long time," Cherry said. "You need to give your mother another call tonight. She will have found him by then."

"I hope you're right."

"I am." Cherry tossed them a knowing smile,

one that said she was always right. Then, when her cell phone rang, she excused herself and walked off to take the call in private.

Blake gave Cindy's hand a gentle squeeze. "You really believe that stuff, don't you?"

"I believe *her.* She was right about so many things."

Blake dropped her hand long enough to slip his arm around her waist and pull her close. "I love you, crazy ideas and all. Now, come on. Let's get a taste of the Gut-Rot before Tuck eats it all."

As they neared the area where the local chili chefs had prepared their specialties, Blake slid a glance at Cindy. "You know, I do believe you're glowing."

"So are you." She tossed him a smile.

With her heart nearly ready to burst with love, and Blake Gray Feather at her side, Cindy was going to shine—not only during the fair, but for the rest of her life.

Because when it came to winning a prize, the heart of a stubborn cowboy beat a blue ribbon any ol' day.

* * * * *